The Daddy Project

Kerri Carpenter

ALLY PRESS

For my cousins—I love you all!

Prologue

"Only ten minutes until midnight."

A cheer sounded in the packed room as people decked out in their best festive outfits and silly party hats applauded another year's ending. Amelia completely agreed with the feeling. She couldn't wait for a new year.

A new life.

She sighed and retreated further back into the corner of the room. She used to love her parents' New Year's Eve parties. It was a chance to catch up with family and friends, celebrate the old year, and anticipate the new one. Plus, she was used to everyone praising her and her life choices.

But this year was different. This year she was as unsteady as the revelers hanging out in Times Square.

The last year hadn't been all bad, she reasoned. After all, her sister, Emerson, had gotten married and was happier than she'd ever seen her. Her roommate Grace got engaged over Christmas.

And just having a roommate was a big deal for her. She'd moved out of her parent's house and into the three-story townhouse in the heart of Old Town Alexandria that her sister and Grace used to share.

Of course, she'd only been at her parent's house because she'd decided to end her six-month-long marriage. More like, six-month *short* marriage. In any case, six months had been six months too many.

Amelia closed her eyes. She should have never married Charlie.

There were a lot of things she shouldn't have done in her life. But interestingly, as she became introspective this holiday season as so many people did, she realized there were even more things she should have done.

But Amelia spent the majority of her life—all twenty-seven years—toeing the line. She did everything that had been expected of her. By her parents, teachers, pageant and cheerleading coaches, sorority sisters, and then her husband. It wasn't as if she'd been unhappy, per se. She'd always considered herself a positive, optimistic person. Excluding these last few months. While she hadn't been unhappy, she hadn't really been happy either. She never did anything for herself. Just her. Just Amelia.

Now she was having a major pity party. Table for one.

She'd been dutiful to first her parents and then her boyfriend-turned-husband. Despite the urge, she'd never taken the time to travel or pursue her own interests.

And whose fault was that, she thought begrudgingly.

"Amelia."

She looked up and couldn't help but smile as her friend and roommate Grace Harris headed in her direction. In a fully bedecked gold and silver party dress, Grace was absolutely glowing. But it wasn't the glitter that gave her that inner sparkle. She'd recently gotten engaged to her boyfriend Xander.

"Are you so excited to start your new job?" Grace asked.

"I am." She was also nervous. Very nervous.

Amelia had been working in the same place since she graduated from college. Her mother's bridal boutique, Dewitt Bridal, located in Old Town Alexandria. In fact, she'd worked there throughout high school and on breaks from college too.

Now, she was venturing out with a job that Grace had helped her secure. She would still be in the wedding world but as an admin and basic office helper. At least, that's how the job was sold to her when she interviewed with Nadine Greene, co-owner of Something True, a new wedding website that was quickly growing in popularity. Having worked in a bridal boutique with thousands of brides, she was very familiar with Something True. In fact, she already had countless ideas for the site. Of course, as the office assistant, she would probably be relegated to more menial tasks. At least, it was a change.

"You're going to do great. When do you start?"

"On the second." She put a hand to her mouth and began to chew on a nail before she remembered that was her worst habit. She dropped her hand. "I don't even know what to wear."

Grace smiled, her eyes shining with kindness. "Don't worry. I'm going to stay at Xander's house tonight. But I'll be home tomorrow around noon, and we'll spend all afternoon and evening finding you the perfect outfit."

She was lucky to live with Grace, even if it wouldn't be lasting much longer since Grace and Xander would be getting married the next fall. Grace was actually her sister's best friend, but she'd always treated Amelia as more than just her BFF's little sister.

"Thanks, Grace."

Grace toasted Amelia with her champagne before she flitted off to her fiancé's side. Grace and Xander were such a great match. Anyone could see their chemistry. She tilted her head as she considered them.

When Grace and Xander were together, love emanated from them. Anyone in the state of Virginia could see how much they were into each other. Had she ever felt that way about anyone?

Speaking of love, her sister and her new brother-in-law walked into the room. Emerson and Jack were simply made for each other. Her sister had been through so much over the last couple of years, and Amelia was happy for her. Yet, that little green hand of jealousy threatened to clasp her heart and squeeze.

She'd wanted that kind of relationship with Charlie. But they'd never come close. Charlie was more concerned with advancing his career and making work contacts. Often times, Amelia got the feeling she could have been running around the house on fire and he wouldn't have noticed.

When she told him she wanted to end their short marriage, he'd seemed surprised. Surprised, but not upset. Not devastated.

"Someone looks deep in thought."

Amelia snapped to attention at her sister's voice. Emerson stood in front of her in a bright pink dress, accessorized with long silver earrings and matching strappy heels.

"I…um…well…"

"Are you okay?" Worry filled Emerson's eyes.

"Yeah, sure," she lied. "I'm happy this year is ending." That part was true enough.

Emerson nodded solemnly. "You've had a rough year." She wrapped Amelia in a long, encouraging hug. "But you know what? I'm proud of you."

Amelia snorted. Then she grabbed her sister's drink and took a sip. "Oh please. What is there to be proud of?"

Emerson took her drink back. "Are you kidding? You moved out of Mom and Dad's house. You just got a new, fabulous job."

"I'm going to be an administrative assistant."

Emerson put her drink down and shook Amelia's shoulders. "At a new startup company. Who knows what kinds of possibilities this could lead to."

"I'm going to be answering the phone, fielding emails, and fetching coffee."

Emerson tilted her head in consideration. "Didn't you mention that you had tons of ideas for the website?"

Amelia shrugged. "All above my pay grade."

Emerson leaned back and peered at her. "You know what you need?"

Amelia narrowed her eyes. "No, but I have a feeling you're going to tell me anyway."

"Just one of the advantages of being an older sister." She pointed a finger at Amelia. "You need to do you."

"Um…"

"Do. You."

"Stop saying that." She scrunched up her nose. "It sounds dirty."

Emerson laughed, her curls bouncing around her head. "It's empowering. Take this next year and do things for you. You now have two things that most people would kill for: time and independence."

She'd always idolized her big sister. Emerson had bucked tradition countless times. She'd gone to the college she'd wanted and started her own company and bought a townhouse. Amelia desperately wished she could be more like that.

"This is your year, Mia. I know it," Emerson said supportively.

"I love that you call me Mia. It makes me feel lighter. Amelia is sooo formal. And I've just never felt that formal, even when I was wearing glitz gowns at pageants. Does that even make sense?"

Emerson laughed. "Not really. But if you like being called Mia, why don't you ask everyone to call you that? It can be part of your transformation. Stop being Amelia and welcome Mia to the fold."

Why didn't she? Seemed so simple when her sister put it like that. She'd been leaning toward changing her last name back to Dewitt. It hadn't seemed right to keep Charlie's last name. It wasn't hers. But Em was right. She could be called whatever she wanted.

Mia. Mia Reynolds. It had a nice ring to it.

"The year of Mia," Emerson said with a wink.

"Guys, come on. It's time." Grace grabbed one of her hands and one of Emerson's and tugged. They laughed and followed her into the living room where most of the party guests were jammed in the room, eyes glued to the countdown on the television.

Could it really be the year of Mia?

Ten, night, eight…

This was a new year. A new her. No more formal, stuffy Amelia. Light, breezy Mia.

Seven, six, five, four…

This year she would do what she wanted and finally, finally live her life.

Three, two, one. Happy New Year!

For the first time, Mia felt excited about a new year.

"Happy New Year," she shouted. And then she added quietly, "To me."

Chapter One

A new year and a new opportunity to be late for work. Although, Lincoln McMann had an in with the boss, considering he *was* the boss.

Still, he hated letting anyone down. And he knew his business partner had probably been in their office since seven. Nadine Washington was nothing if not a workaholic. This whole wedding website had been her idea.

He'd hemmed and hawed when she'd first pitched the idea of a website designed to accommodate brides in the Washington, DC-area specifically. What in the world did he know about brides or weddings? But Nadine had been adamant.

"What do you have to lose, Linc?"

He raised an eyebrow.

"You're more than set financially after selling your first website. The custody situation is under control. Finally," she added.

"The twins—" he began.

"Are fine, Linc. Hadley and Hugo are just fine. Sitting at home every day, wringing your fingers together like some kind of old-fashioned damsel, is not going to help them adjust to not having a mother in their lives. You need a job, and this is a great idea."

"But I don't really get the idea. I don't know anything about weddings."

"Who cares? You're the technical brains. You know computers and coding and IT and other super-smart techie stuff. That's what landed you on the cover of that tech magazine."

Actually, the acquisition of his previous website was what did that.

"You don't need to know about weddings," Nadine continued. "That's my job. You will make all of my ideas functional and pretty. We'll be partners, fifty-fifty."

So, he'd acquiesced. Truthfully, he'd never had a chance. Nadine was more than a friend. He'd known her most of his life. She was his mom's best friend. Still was, only his mom and dad had retired and moved down to Florida. Even at twenty-eight years old, Nadine was like a second mother to him.

Linc turned down the alley behind the office space they were renting on the corner of Union and Prince Streets, in the heart of Old Town. He parked in one of their allotted spaces, grabbed his computer case, and stepped out of the car. The early January wind whipping off the Potomac River immediately made his eyes water. He hustled around the building, ignoring the commuters heading to work, honking car horns, and screeching breaks of public buses.

He pushed through the front door, and, as expected, found Nadine already at her desk, staring straight ahead at her computer screen as her hand hovered over her mouse.

"Sorry I'm late," he said with a grimace and what he hoped was an apologetic look.

"No problem. There aren't any fires to put out."

"Yet." He walked around Nadine's desk and continued to his large workspace.

"Hey, you've created a problem-free product. This website runs like a well-oiled machine."

He dumped his stuff on his desk, removed his coat and hat, and began turning on all his different computers. He checked the main server and was getting ready to go through the usual reports when a cup of coffee appeared on his desk. He looked up to find Nadine wearing a knowing grin.

"What?" he asked. "And thank you for this." He took a sip of the dark roast coffee and savored the caffeine.

"You seem frazzled," she said. "I mean, more frazzled than normal."

He reached for a framed picture of his son and daughter. God, they were adorable, he thought. He loved them so much. Even on mornings like this when adorable was not quite the word he'd use to describe them. "I thought it was the terrible twos. More like the frenetic fours."

"How are my favorite twins?"

"They seem to like doing the same thing, only at different times. Today, Hadley was a perfect little angel and Hugo was her devilish counterpart."

"Uh-oh. What did he do?"

14

"What didn't he do?" Linc replaced the photo. "It was a Cheerios-up-the-nose-kind-of-morning."

"Well, it's a new year," Nadine said, propping a hip on the corner of his desk.

"I heard that somewhere." He winked at her.

"Shut up, smarty pants."

"Plus, there were other signs of the year changing. Let's see, there were all the messages on Facebook that clued me in. Then I turned on the TV just in time to see the ball drop in New York. Plus, I heard all of the crazy drunk people celebrating outside my house."

"That's what you get for living so close to the heart of Old Town." Nadine wagged a finger at him.

"Didn't say I was complaining. Only that I spotted the whole new year thing."

"Did you spot that it's time for you to embrace the new year and maybe make some resolutions?"

Linc took a longer gulp of his coffee. The hot liquid burned his throat, but he'd rather do that than have this same old conversation with Nadine.

"Fine, I'll stop smoking," he said.

Nadine narrowed her big brown eyes. "You don't smoke."

"I'll drink less."

Her hands went to her hips. "I'm sure that one whole beer a week will really miss you."

"How about I vow to lose weight?" he asked with a wink.

She slapped his chest. "You are in perfect shape, despite the fact that you sit behind that computer all day." She sighed. Loudly. "I was talking to your mom last night."

15

Here we go.

"We only want you to be happy."

He'd also spoken to his parents recently and knew exactly where Nadine was heading. "Okay, then. I did make a resolution," Linc said. Nadine's brows went up. "I made a resolution to work from home more."

Nadine rolled her eyes. "How about you resolve to go on some dates or get a social life? You know all those New Year's revelers you heard the other night? They were coming from bars and restaurants that are right near your house."

"How astute of you to notice."

She poked him in the chest. "You could be one of the revelers. When was the last time you even got dressed up? Probably when I forced you to take those headshots for the website."

She was the creative genius behind Something True and he was the IT guy. Well, he was a little more than that. After graduating in three years from MIT, Linc had a plethora of job opportunities. He'd passed over all of them in favor of starting an IT company with his college roommate. The company did well and when they sold it to an even larger tech giant, Linc had been left sitting pretty in the cash department.

Money had been the only thing that had gone right for him in the last couple of years.

He'd married young, but he'd been so enamored with his college sweetheart—also his first serious girlfriend—that he'd never stood a chance. She was the one to suggest they elope. He'd gone along for the ride.

He used to love her impulsiveness. Weekend getaways decided on Friday afternoons, parties thrown at the drop of a hat, major life decisions made over a second glass of tequila. The warning signs were all there. But he'd been too foolish to see them.

Then Chrissy found out she was pregnant. Linc had been terrified. Being twenty-four and finding out you were going to be a dad was crazy enough. But to find out you were going to be a dad two times over, now that was an eye-opener.

In the end it didn't matter. The first time he'd held those two little wiggling, red-faced bundles of joy in the hospital, he'd been a total goner. He couldn't even imagine his life without Hadley and Hugo.

Everything had been going perfect in his life. Twin babies, a great job that had started garnering some serious interest in the tech world, and a happy wife. Only, Chrissy hadn't been happy. He figured that out when she left him and the kids with only a note explaining her actions.

I can't do this. I can't be this tied down. I wasn't meant to be a mother. Sorry, Linc.

Sorry. Like that was going to help his life that had just been upended. It hadn't lasted though. By the next summer, Chrissy returned, claiming she was a new person. She'd changed. She was ready to settle down now.

They reconciled. Everything had been perfect. Until Fall.

Chrissy couldn't even make it to Thanksgiving before she took off again. Linc had enough. He served her with divorce papers, something that apparently shocked Chrissy. That's when the lawyers had to get involved. Then Linc sold his company and became a very wealthy man. That's when the custody trial

17

happened. He'd never taken Chrissy for a gold digger, but she'd wanted the kids, so she could get Linc's child support.

After a long period of fighting, court, judges, and money, everything ended. Chrissy's true personality came out in court, and no judge was going to put the care of young twins in her incapable hands.

She took off after that. He had no idea where she'd gone.

"Hello."

He looked up into Nadine's kind, chocolate eyes. He couldn't believe he'd gone down that rabbit hole.

"Sorry, what?" he asked.

"So, I have this friend…" Nadine began.

"No, no, no." He emphatically shook his head. "No blind dates. Actually, no dates at all." He considered himself completely off the market.

"Linc, you aren't even thirty yet. You need to get out there and date."

"What I need is to focus on my children and this job."

"From nine to five, you focus on work. As for your kids, Hadley and Hugo aren't going to be devastated if you take a couple of hours to have dinner with someone. In fact, I'll even babysit for you."

"No."

She squeezed his shoulder. "Just think about it."

"No."

"I really hate you. You know that?"

Linc grinned. "No, you don't."

Nadine grinned. "True. Oh, by the way, our new office assistant is starting today."

"Thanks for taking the lead on hiring someone."

"No problem. I'd much rather hire an employee than code or rewire or debug or whatever it is that you do." Nadine walked back toward her desk. "I am going to keep irritating you about dating though."

He knew it. Linc sighed. After what he'd been through with Chrissy, he felt emotionally traumatized. "Nadine, I just want to live an easy, noncomplicated existence with a little stability, calm, and order. And no surprises," he added for good measure.

They both turned at the sound of the front door opening. A tall woman crossed the threshold. As she did, the hair on the back of Linc's neck stood up. He leaned forward.

"Um, hi," the woman said. "I'm the new assistant."

Linc and Nadine both rose, and Nadine walked over to greet the woman. She looked so familiar to him. She had light red hair. Was it auburn or maybe strawberry blonde? He wasn't sure. And the way she carried herself was with confidence and grace. She was stately and beautiful. She actually looked like...

No. No way. This woman couldn't be...

She turned toward Linc. Nadine introduced them. "Linc, this is Amelia—"

"Dewitt," he finished for her. "You're Amelia Dewitt." His first crush. The girl he'd held as the epitome of perfection. He'd loved her from afar through most of his childhood and adolescence.

As he continued to take her in, his earlier statement ran through his head. Any chance of life not getting complicated just flew out the window.

***

There were a lot of things Mia expected to happen on her first day of work. Filling out paperwork, getting acclimated with the computer files and email system. She might even need to grab lunch or coffee for her new bosses.

But she had definitely not anticipated running into someone she knew. Or, someone who knew her. Because as far as Mia was concerned, she had no idea who she was dealing with.

That was too bad though since this guy was seriously cute. He wasn't her usual type, but there was something about his slightly disheveled demeanor that screamed yummy.

And he was still staring at her. Amelia felt her face blush.

"It's actually Amelia Reynolds now," she said, correcting him from using her maiden name. Then she remembered her New Year's resolution. "Oh, and actually, just call me Mia."

"Mia, it is," Nadine said, looking back and forth between her and the staring man.

"It's been a really long time since I saw you," he said.

Mia froze. She quickly tried to take stock of the guy. Where did he know her from? This guy knew her maiden name and had said it had been a while since he saw her.

Apparently realizing she was at a loss, he stepped forward, hand extended. He hit his hip against one of the desks. "Ow. Linc," he said, placing a hand on his chest. He coughed. "Uh, Lincoln McMann. We went to high school together. And middle school. And the last couple years of elementary school."

"Lincoln McMann…" Finally, she remembered. Lincoln McMann. Smart kid who usually sat in the back corner. He never raised his hands, but if he was called on, he always knew the right answer. He had been a total computer genius back then. Mia had been a great student, usually pulling in A's and B's. But Lincoln McMann had been on a whole other level.

She glanced around the space and took in the multiple computers next to where Linc had been standing. Seems like he was still the computer genius. She remembered he'd gotten into a really good college; maybe an Ivy or MIT. But she hadn't heard what happened to him after that.

"Ohmigod," she said, shaking his hand. "I'm so sorry, Lincoln."

"Uh, just Linc."

"Linc. I apologize for not recognizing you. You're right. It has been a long time. How are you? You work here? Obviously." She shook her head.

Nadine spoke up. "Linc and I are partners. He's the IT wiz I told you about during your interview."

"Oh, right," she said dumbly.

"I just handle the computers. Nadine basically keeps everything else rolling. Without her, there would be no Something True."

This was probably more words than Linc had spoken to her during all four years of high school.

"Linc has always been overly modest." Nadine patted him on the shoulder. "Why don't I give you a tour of our office? It won't take long. The office isn't much, but it's been a great place to start the business."

"Sounds good," Mia said, removing her coat.

She hadn't been sure what to wear for her first day. In her mother's bridal boutique, they always wore all-black outfits so as not to take away from the brides and gowns. With Grace's help, she'd chosen tailored black slacks that flared at her ankles, black booties, and a deep teal silk blouse that Grace claimed brought out the blue of her eyes.

Now, looking at Linc's worn jeans and sweater and Nadine's tunic top—and were those yoga pants?—Mia feared she may be a tad overdressed.

Nadine took Mia's coat and hung it on a rack near the door. Mia stood there awkwardly, desperately wanting to bite her nails.

"Is what I'm wearing okay?" she asked tentatively. She was just glad she'd nixed the suit jacket she'd considered bringing.

"You look amazing," Linc said, shoving his hands in his pockets.

Nadine returned and gave Linc a small shove. "Go play with your computers." She focused her attention on Mia. "You do look great, but don't feel like you need to dress up. It's just the three of us here. Wear whatever makes you feel comfortable."

"Got it."

"Great. Now, this is your desk." Nadine showed her the desk situated closest to the door. "You are going to have quite a big job here. We are hoping to expand soon, and we need help with pretty much everything."

Mia placed her Kate Spade on the ergonomic chair and ran her hand over the desk. Wow, her very own desk area complete with computer, phone, drawers, filing cabinets, and tons of office supplies. She knew most people wouldn't be excited by such stuff, but for her, this was basically her first job. She really couldn't remember a time when she hadn't worked at her mom's store.

She allowed a moment for the pride to wash over her.

"Besides assisting Linc and myself, you'll be acting as the receptionist."

"Do you get many visitors?" she asked.

"Hardly ever. But we do get a fair amount of deliveries. You'll come to know the UPS and FedEx men quite well."

It was a shame they didn't get more people in the office. The space was absolutely lovely. Small and cozy but decorated very simply. The walls were painted a very light blue-gray and the floors were a gray laminate. The best part of the space was the fact that there were large windows on almost every wall, allowing natural light in. Plus, they had a great view of the Potomac River and Waterfront Park. That means they would get to see all of the beautiful Cherry Blossom trees in the Spring.

"We have a break area over here," Nadine said, showing her a room with a circular table, four chairs, and a long counter with shelves above it. There was a Keurig, a filtered water machine, a sink, microwave, toaster oven, and a small fridge. "You can bring your lunch or go out. There are a ton of restaurants in Old Town."

"I actually live—"

"Oh, yes, that's right," Nadine said. "You live a couple blocks from here."

She continued the tour. Mia saw where they kept supplies, the copy room, and the restrooms. Back in the main office, Linc basically took up one side of the room with a very large desk and about twenty different computer screens. Well, maybe not that many, but more than Mia had ever seen. On the wall behind him hung three framed posters of the original *Star Wars* movies. Nadine was on the other wall. Her area was happily decorated with a vase and fresh flowers, a cute floral wall calendar, picture frames, and other colorful trinkets.

"What should I work on first?" Mia asked.

"I'd like to tell you a little more about the business, but…" She trailed off as she glanced at her computer screen. "I have a conference call that I have to take in five minutes. Hm…. Hey, Linc?"

Linc looked up, pushing his glasses further up his nose. "What's up?"

"Can you go over Something True with Mia while I take this call? And explain what you do over there."

"Uh, sure." He began to stand and knocked over a coffee mug in the process. Luckily, it appeared the mug was empty.

Mia stifled a giggle and walked over to Linc's space.

"Take a seat." Linc pulled a second chair toward his desk.

She dutifully sat down. Mia could only describe Linc's workspace as organized chaos. There were binders and notebooks, a couple pairs of intense looking headphones, lots of cords and other gadgets she couldn't quite identify. While her fingers itched to make orderly piles of his tech treasures, she could somehow tell that Linc knew where every single thing was located. And in his mind, it all made sense.

"Something True is a website devoted to the Washington, DC-area. Anything and everything specific to weddings in this region can be found on our site. The plan is to expand to other parts of the country over the next couple of years.

"I'm actually pretty familiar with Something True," she said. His went brows up. "I worked at Dewitt Bridal for my mom. We used your site a lot with our brides."

"That's fantastic."

"I'm happy to hear you and Nadine are planning on expanding. We had a ton of out-of-town people—other brides, bridesmaids, and relatives—wish they had a similar site where they lived."

Linc seemed really pleased to hear that. In fact, a slight red tinted his cheeks. He went on to start explaining his specific function at the company. She followed along until he started using phrases like *HTML* and *coding on the backend*. Mia bit her lip and nodded her head as if she knew exactly what he was talking about. Her knowledge of HTML coding was limited to very basic skills.

Damn, Linc McMann was hella smart. And good-looking.

Now she was the one doing the staring. But Mia was trying to reconcile the shy kid from high school with the competent man standing before her.

She remembered he had been one of the taller guys in their class. But he'd been super-skinny and kinda gawky. Now, he'd filled out, grown into that height. It appeared that beneath his gray sweater, he was actually kind of buff.

His hair probably needed a trim, she mused. It was sandy-blonde, with a bit of a wave. She wondered if it grew much longer if it would start to curl.

"You know what I mean?" he asked, pointing at a black tower next to one of his screens.

"Ah, yep." She literally had no idea what he was talking about. But something about his last statement must have excited him because his light brown eyes were practically dancing with excitement.

She'd never really been one for glasses but seeing how they looked on Linc might just have her changing her mind. He wore black-rimmed frames that were a little too loose and kept sliding down his nose. It was adorable.

Mia shook her head. When was the last time she'd thought anyone was adorable or cute? She'd been walking around in a fog since her marriage ended. Right now, the opposite sex was something that didn't hold any appeal to her. No matter how attractive they were.

Not to mention, she really couldn't think about Linc like that. He was her boss, for goodness sake. Dating between coworkers was explicitly forbidden. Wasn't it?

Now that she thought about it, she really didn't know. She'd worked in a bridal boutique where her colleagues consisted of her mother, other women, and a couple gay guys. These kinds of thoughts would have involved a major lifestyle change.

Yet, she couldn't stop her mind from going right across that one-foot gap to Linc's irresistible grin, those sweet eyes, and sexy glasses. She'd love to run her hands through his floppy hair. Even though she'd kind of sworn off dating for the next decade or so, it was kinda nice to feel that little flutter of a crush in her belly. Besides, nothing could ever happen between her and her boss. So where was the harm in looking?

Linc said something and then gestured, knocking over a picture as he did. She grabbed the silver frame and flipped it over. A young boy and girl, both with heads of golden curls, stared back at her. What was more, they had the same goofy grin as Linc. Their dad?

"That's my son and daughter," he confirmed. He pointed to the girl. "This is Hadley and her brother Hugo. They're four now."

"Twins?"

"Yep."

"Oh." *Real insightful comment, Mia.* Stupid, stupid Mia. He was married. Of course, he was. He was a total catch. "Do you have a picture of your wife too?" she asked, trying to be a good sport.

"Um, actually." He held his left hand up. It took her a moment, but Mia realized his ring finger was bare. "I'm divorced."

"Oh," she repeated.

"Yeah, my ex isn't really in the picture anymore. Hadley and Hugo live with me full time."

Oh wow. A super-smart, cute computer genius who was a single father to four-year-old twins. She felt like a balloon with a leak. She deflated as her thoughts of a safe, untouchable crush evaporated.

She'd just have to concentrate on her new job and her new life. She was ready to try new things and have fun adventures. Linc was on a completely different path.

She'd stay in her lane and wave to him as she passed by.

Chapter Two

Shortly after five o'clock, Mia donned her winter coat, hat, and gloves, and left the office. Her first day of work complete. She let out a grateful sigh.

After her initial crush-like feelings about Linc, she'd been able to get down to work organizing invoices. Well, mostly. She may have still given him a glance or two. But she did not have any more thoughts on dating or kissing him.

Okay, she had a couple thoughts. After all, he was *really* cute.

She sighed loudly but knew it would go unnoticed as she walked the streets of Old Town. There were too many noises and other distractions. It was one of the many things she loved about this area. Especially after having lived in the suburbs her whole life.

Old Town was a part of Alexandria, Virginia, a DC-suburb that was located across the Potomac River from the capital. It was a fun area that attracted both tourists and locals of all ages. Mia had grown up not far from Old Town, down the George Washington Parkway in a neighborhood near Mount Vernon. She couldn't believe she'd waited until she was twenty-seven to move to the center of Alexandria.

There were restaurants and bars galore. Visitors could get any kind of food they were looking for, including homemade custard, specialty doughnuts, and more. Plus, there were wonderful shops everywhere; anything from trendy chains to unique mom-and-pop stores. She loved strolling the uneven red brick sidewalks, popping in to one shop after another.

Twinkly lights were strung along the trees that lined the streets. Some of those streets were still cobblestone. It gave Old Town an interesting feel. The present marrying the past. There was so much history here, she thought as she walked past the Stabler-Leadbeater Apothecary Museum. She knew if she stepped inside, she would be transported back into the nineteenth century.

As she continued walking, she was tempted to turn onto King Street, the main drag of Old Town, and stop at one of the many bars for a much-needed glass of wine. Or maybe a stronger drink. But she knew her sister and Grace were anxiously awaiting her return home, so they could hear all about her first day.

She continued walking the few blocks to the townhouse, passing other people leaving work for the day. Some were heading toward bus stops or the Metro. Others were off to have those strong drinks on King Street.

Mia reveled in the fact that she was a commuter now, even if that commute was only a couple block walk. She actually enjoyed the hustle and bustle of the streets. She didn't mind hearing the car horns and screeching buses and other traffic. It may not last, but for the moment, she was thrilled she was getting to walk in the frigid cold air after a day in the office. They were supposed to get snow tonight. She wondered if that would actually happen.

"Mia, you're home," her sister screamed from the front stoop of the townhouse she owned. Mia had just turned the corner.

Emerson had bought the townhouse with her ex-fiancé. After he called off their wedding, Emerson had converted the bottom floor into offices for her event planning firm and her best friend, Grace's, wedding planning business. Emerson and Grace then moved into the two upstairs' floors. Now that Emerson was a married woman and living with her husband, Mia had taken her spot.

"Hurry up and get over here," Emerson called. "I'm freezing."

"Then why are you outside without a coat, crazy woman," Mia yelled back with a laugh.

Finally, she made it to the house and put her arm around her sister as they shuffled inside.

"Come into my office," Emerson said, steering Mia to the left. "Grace is stuck on a call with a bride who is standing dangerously close to the proverbial edge. Too bad for her because I want to hear everything."

Emerson grabbed two bottles of water out of a mini-fridge she kept in the office. Then they settled down onto the loveseat that was situated in front of the bay window.

"So," Emerson said, her blue eyes lighting up with excitement. "Tell me everything. How did it go?"

"Well," Mia began. An image of Linc popped into her mind. "It was mostly good."

"Mostly?" Emerson wrinkled her nose. "First days are always hard. You probably didn't sleep great last night with all the anxiety and nerves of beginning something new."

She hit the nail on the head. At least, half the nail. Mia nodded.

"Do you think you'll be able to do the job well?"

"I do," Mia said honestly. "There will be a decent amount of invoice processing and handling. I took care of all of that for mama, so I'm not worried about it."

"Plus, you must be familiar with the website."

"I am. It's a great resource for local brides."

"Did you tell your new boss about any of your ideas?"

Mia let out a mirthless laugh. "Em, it was my first day. Besides, I'm a simple office assistant. I think my boss knows what she's doing."

"But if you have an idea that could help the website..." Emerson trailed off, probably at the look Mia shot in her direction. "All I'm saying is that you have really great instincts, Mia. Trust them."

Mia's response to this was to blow her hair out of her face and chug half the bottle of water.

"How many coworkers? Grace said it was a small operation."

"It's just me and my two bosses, the cofounders of the site."

Emerson waited, watching her with expectant eyes. "And? How are they?"

31

"Um, great. Yeah. They're nice. Nadine is the one who hired me."

Emerson sat back. Her eyes narrowed. "Why do I feel like there's a 'but' coming? Or, something that didn't sit well with you."

Mia fidgeted on the couch. She decided to ignore her sister's comment. Instead, she asked, "Do you remember someone named Lincoln McMann from school?"

"Linc?" Emerson asked. "Of course. God, that guy was smart. Funny too, if you could get him talking."

"You talked to him?"

Emerson nodded. "Sure. He was in a couple of my classes."

Emerson had been two years ahead of Mia in school. But it was no surprise Linc had been bumped up to take more advanced classes.

"Why are you asking about Linc McMann?"

"He's my new boss," Mia said. "He's the IT brains of the operation."

"How funny. What a small world. It must have been nice to see him," Emerson said earnestly.

"The thing is, I didn't recognize him. Once he told me who he was, I remembered him. But, I didn't really talk to him in high school."

"Does he still wear those glasses?" Emerson asked.

Those sexy glasses that made her heartrate pick up? "Yeah. I'm assuming they're not the same exact pair."

Mia didn't want to talk about Linc any longer. He was her boss and he was a father, and she was just beginning to figure out who she wanted to be. So that was that.

"Anyway, I have a whole desk area to myself. I'm going to be answering the phone and helping with general emails. Plus, I have to order office supplies, and…what?"

Emerson was watching her with a very questioning expression. She pointed at Mia and swirled her finger around. "I don't know. Something is happening in there." She tapped Mia on the head.

"Like you said, I didn't sleep much last night and it was a long day."

"Hm." That was all Emerson would say, but she continued studying her.

"Emerson, you're starting to creep me out."

"Is Linc still a cutie pie?"

Mia tilted her head. "You thought Linc was attractive in high school?"

"Sure. I mean, he wasn't your traditional jock and he definitely wasn't a pretty boy. But he had this sort of beta male Harry Potter chic thing about him."

"Harry Potter chic?" Mia chuckled. "He's…cute. I guess."

"You guess, huh?" Emerson grinned.

Mia groaned. Her sister had totally caught her. "It doesn't matter how cute he is, I am a divorcee."

Emerson rolled her eyes. "Don't be so dramatic. You are simply a woman who married the wrong guy. And what's this about Linc being cute?"

"I…uh…I mean," she stuttered. "You were the one who said he was cute first."

"I said he was cute in high school. But you saw him today and thought he was cute. There's a difference."

"It does not matter," Mia repeated. "He's my boss. And he has kids."

"He's married?"

"Divorced. With two kids. Twins."

"So, what? You like kids. And twins? How sweet!"

"Emerson! It's not sweet. He's my boss who is a single dad so I can't have a safe crush on him."

"A safe crush?"

"Yeah, you know, an untouchable crush."

Mia shook her head. "Huh?"

"Like when you think someone is attractive, but they are totally off-limits. Like a married man or a priest."

"Ohhhhh." Emerson laughed. "I get it. It's okay to look but not touch."

"Exactly."

"There's just one issue here. Why would Linc be off-limits? You said he's divorced."

"He's my boss."

"Hm." That was all her sister said in response.

"Emerson! You're not implying that I should start something up with my new boss, are you?"

"I thought you wanted to start fresh this year. Be a new you. Have adventures and start living."

"I do, but I don't think ogling after my boss is the best way to go about achieving that."

"Ogling, huh?" Emerson laughed again. Mia threw a throw pillow at her.

"Shut up."

Emerson continued to laugh. Grace entered the room then, practically sashaying in her magenta sweater dress and tall boots. Grace could give any model a run for their money.

"What'd I miss?" Grace asked.

"Mia is lusting after her boss."

"Oohhh," Grace said and wiggled her eyebrows.

"I am not lusting. I just think he's good-looking. And you're not helping," she said to her sister.

"What do you want me to say?"

Mia thought about it while Grace pulled one of the desk chairs over and plopped down in it. "I want you to say, 'Mia, this is a new job and you have to act professionally. It doesn't matter how attractive your boss is.'"

Grace whistled. "Now we're getting to the good stuff."

The good stuff was exactly what Mia was afraid of.

***

"Be good," Linc called after his kids as they ran toward their playroom with Josh, one of their friends from nursery school.

Playdates made him nervous, because adding even one more child to his life was terrifying. But he owed pretty much every parent in the twins' school. How many times had they helped him out with Hugo and Hadley? If Josh's mom needed a sitter for one hour, the least he could do was help her out.

He hung the kids' coats and hats up on their hooks by the door. Then he went through their lunch boxes, discarding trash, and wiping them out for the next day. This year they were enrolled in half-day nursery school. They spent the afternoon at their babysitter, Joley's, house. Joley, otherwise known as his godsend, was fantastic with them. He'd offered to have her move into his house. There was a great setup in his basement with an extra bedroom, bathroom, separate entrance, and even a small kitchen. But Joley was happy where she was. Lucky for him, she only lived a couple blocks away.

After he cleaned up the dishes from their rushed breakfast that morning, he peeked in on the kids. All was well in the playroom, also known as the formal dining room. Who needed a dining room table when you could have a sliding board, a pop-up tunnel, and every other toy ever invented.

He grinned as he watched Hadley serve the plastic food she made on her small kitchen to her brother and Josh. He'd get to be a grown up again someday. In the meantime, he would enjoy the Fisher Price kitchen, the *Sesame Street* stuffed animals, and the *Paw Patrol* bike in his dining room. Not to mention the rubber duckies in his bathroom. Or the Dr. Seuss books that hid his collection of Tolkien and Asimov on the bookshelves.

The kids would only be four once and Linc wanted to enjoy every moment. He walked back to the kitchen and considered cracking a beer. Instead, he went with a Diet Coke.

He couldn't believe Chrissy didn't want to be part of this. She'd tried to get custody, but that had been more to get at him, then get her children. She didn't want to be a mother. He'd never understand it.

While the kids may have entered his life a bit earlier than he'd anticipated, he was thrilled to be a parent. He enjoyed doing all the things with them that his own amazing father had done with him. Even if he did struggle somewhat with relating to Hadley, he thought he was getting into the groove with all of her feminine desires such as princess costumes, American Girl Dolls, and glitter on everything.

For a moment, he didn't know what to do with himself. The playroom was calm, the dishes were done, and he was alone. Not a good place to be when all he really wanted was to think about was how someone from his past was now front and center in his present. Luckily, the doorbell rang, and he walked down the hall to answer it.

"Aren't you sick of me yet?" he said as he opened the door to Nadine. She thrust a covered casserole dish into his hands.

"I'm always sick of you. However, I made you a lasagna over the weekend. Here you go."

He smiled. Nadine had been mothering him since the divorce. At first, he thought his own mother had put her up to it. But as time went on, he realized Nadine just had a good heart and she'd been worried about him and the twins.

Speaking of the kids, they ran out to greet Aunt Nadine, dancing excitedly around her. As always, she made a big fuss over them until they were satisfied. Then they happily returned to the playroom. Nadine followed him into the kitchen.

"I can't stay long. I don't want to be late for my belly dancing class."

Linc raised an eyebrow. "Seriously? You're taking belly dancing now?"

"Keeps me young."

"Whatever you say. Maybe I should try it." He attempted to roll his hips around but ended up bumping into the counter.

"Trust me, you don't need to try it. You're young enough. You're still a baby."

"I don't know. Sometimes I feel pretty old and ragged."

"Please." Nadine waved a dismissive hand. "Bake this on three-fifty for forty-five minutes with the foil on. Then remove it and bake for another ten or fifteen until the cheese bubbles. Throw a salad together too. Those kids need their greens."

"Hugo's in a no-green stuff phase. Besides, I don't think I have any lettuce or anything."

Nadine held up a reusable shopping bag. "There's some in here. Plus, those baby carrots I know Hugo likes. And I baked chocolate chip cookies for Hadley's sweet tooth."

"You spoil us." He kissed her on the cheek.

"That's my job."

"I thought your job was running a wedding website." He gestured with a bottle of water, but Nadine shook her head.

"Speaking of work," she began.

Here we go. Linc leaned back against the counter and waited for what he knew was coming.

"I think Mia is going to be a good addition to the office. She catches on quick."

"I guess," he said tentatively.

"Funny that you guys went to the same high school."

So what if Amelia Dewitt, or Mia Reynolds as she was called now, had come back into his life? It didn't really matter since she was working for him. Even if she was interested in him romantically—which she obviously never would be—nothing would ever happen between the two of them. Linc simply couldn't fathom being with someone in a romantic capacity again. Not after Chrissy. Not after everything that happened.

But damn if Mia wasn't the most beautiful woman he'd ever seen. He'd thought that back when he was a teenager and he still did now.

He'd always loved the color of her hair and was happy to see it hadn't changed, although she cut it a little shorter now. It fell around her face in soft layers.

She had light blue eyes that really stood out due to her peaches and cream skin. And while most of the features on her face were delicate, almost regal-looking, she had these really amazing full lips. Linc used to watch her apply this light red lip gloss in high school. She'd take out this compact mirror and pucker up her lips as she studied herself.

He'd always wondered what that lip gloss would taste like? It had smelled like strawberries. He remembered that from their junior year English class. She'd sat right next to him that year. Then again, maybe the gloss was cherry flavored.

"I think the call with New Orleans went well," Nadine was saying.

"Yeah, me too," he said distractedly as he pondered if they made lip gloss in watermelon or pomegranate flavors.

"Going with Nola over Manhattan as our next site is definitely more manageable."

"Yep."

"After reviewing the stats the city bureau provided, they are seeing a huge influx of weddings there."

"Yeah." Then again, he was allergic to pomegranate.

"Mia is really pretty."

"Yes." Linc shook his head and met Nadine's cocky grin. "What did you just say?"

"Oh, Linc. You are so obvious."

"What are you talking about?" He tried his best to ask the question as nonchalantly as possible.

"You ran into how many things today? Dropped how many items?"

He waved his finger back and forth. "I always run into things because I've always been clumsy."

"True. But you were extra clumsy today. And it was all because of Mia. I have never seen you so attentive before. You normally shrink back into your den of computer screens when someone comes into the office. Today, I saw you more than ever."

"What do you want me to do? You hired my high school crush."

"I didn't know she was your high school crush."

Linc shrugged. "Well, she was."

"Was?" Nadine asked, with a knowing stare.

"I'm not in high school anymore."

"No, you're not. Neither is she. In fact, you are both adults. Two unattached, recently divorced adults who are free to date anyone you so choose."

He grumbled. "Not this again."

"Yes, this. I just want to see you happy."

He ran a hand through his hair and wondered when he'd had a haircut last. He was probably overdue for one. "I am happy."

Wasn't he?

The truth was, Linc was on autopilot. He had been for the last two years. Sure, he'd like to go on a date now and then, or even go out for a beer with a buddy. But his kids came first. Making a safe life and dedicated routine for them took priority over everything else. He grew up knowing what time dinner would be and that his dad would always be there to play soccer in the backyard while his mom messed around with her gardens. He wanted his kids to have the same experience.

Adding dating into the mix was something he simply didn't think he could handle. Since he knew Nadine, he was well aware she wouldn't let this go.

"I'm not going to deny that Mia is beautiful. She always has been. And she's smart too. But I'm not going to date someone I work with." *I'm not going to date anyone at all.* "Besides, she was always out of my league."

"Interesting, since she was checking you out today. I kept catching her glancing over at you."

Really? Was Nadine being serious? Had the homecoming queen checked out the computer nerd? Did it matter?

Determined, he gave a curt nod. "That's nice to hear. But nothing is going to happen there."

"Linc—"

"However, I will consider being a little more social."

Nadine's hand flew to her chest. "Really?"

Not with dating. He just couldn't. But, it wouldn't kill him to go out for some beers with friends. Or maybe catch a baseball game when the weather was nicer. "Yes. But you have to let me do it in my own time and in my own way. And I will take you up on the babysitting offer."

She hugged him tightly. "Sounds good, sugar." With that, she left for her belly dancing class.

41

Linc stood in the kitchen dumbly. What had just happened here? Somehow Nadine finagled him to agree to a social life. A social life he really didn't want at the moment. Not that he would mind going out with a woman.

Someone friendly and warm.

Someone who liked children.

Someone who got his heart beating.

Someone like Mia. The girl he'd been half in love with most of his life.

"Linc, you are ridiculous. Never. Gonna. Happen," he said into the kitchen.

There were a million women out there. It wouldn't do any good to think of the one who was working five feet away.

As far as he was concerned, it wasn't that Mia was off-limits to him. It was that Linc was off-limits to everyone.

Chapter Three

There were mornings that moved like clockwork, where everything was smooth sailing.

This was not one of those mornings.

Linc woke up to three inches of snow on the ground. Not really a lot in snow standards, but for the DC-area, it was crippling. The government hadn't shut down, but most of the local schools were operating on a two-hour delay. Since the twins went to a nursery school for a couple hours in the morning, a delay meant that school was canceled all together.

He'd frantically called Joley. Unfortunately, Joley's mother had slipped on those three inches and injured her back. Joley was taking her to the doctor's office.

He'd tried his Aunt Cicely, who loved to watch the twins. But she'd flown down to visit his parents in Florida for the month. She wanted to escape the cold. Smart lady.

Linc put in call after call to various babysitters and neighbors to no avail. In the meantime, Hadley had decided to move on from cooking plastic food to real food. Linc found a flood of milk on the kitchen floor with some Cheerios bobbing around like little life preservers.

Speaking of life preservers, that's really what Linc could use. Or maybe he needed something else. Someone else. A partner. A wife.

We're fine. We're fine. We're fine. Many times over the last two years he'd repeated this mantra to himself. Realistically, he knew that they were fine. But when everything was going wrong, it was hard to remember.

He could handle all of this. He *would* handle it. But damn, it would be nice to have someone else. Not only to clean up the spilled milk and figure out child care, but to share his concerns with. Someone who wanted this life with cereal on the floor and two young kids to raise.

Whenever Nadine brought up dating or getting a social life, these were the moments he wanted her to see. So she could understand why he was hesitant to bring someone into this. Was there even a woman out there who wanted this too? And if there was, would he ever be able to trust someone again?

Hugo had had an accident early in the morning and Linc was running around stripping his bed and calming his son down. "Hugo, it was an accident. Everybody has them. Remember, Hadley had one a couple weeks ago." And she'd been just as upset as Hugo.

Finally, one of the parents of Hugo's friends said she could watch them. But not until eleven. He could make that work.

He'd simply work from home in the morning. With the kids at home, he knew he wouldn't get much done, but at least he would be online in case the weather or anything else affected the servers.

He cleaned up the kitchen, started the laundry with Hugo's sheets, and settled down in the kitchen to work. That's when the lights went out.

"You've got to be kidding me." He ran a hand through his hair.

"Daddy, I can't see," Hadley called from the playroom.

"I know, sweetie. I think the power went out."

"Can I go out and play in the snow?" Hugo asked.

"No, not right now."

"But whyyyyyy?"

"Because." His parents used to answer him that way often and he usually accepted it. His kids, however, did not.

"Because why?"

Linc ignored Hugo and walked to the front of the house. He peered out the window and saw dark houses all up and down the street. Great, a power outage.

His cell phone rang just as Hugo screamed, "I want to build a snowman."

"Daddy, can I watch Frozen?" Hadley asked, dancing around his legs.

"No, sweetie, the power's out. That means the television won't work." Hadley was staying close to him. She never liked being in the dark.

He saw Nadine's office number on his cell and quickly answered. "Nadine, what's going on? Is the power out there too?"

"No, the power is still on, but something is going on with the website. I think the server's down."

"Dammit."

"Daddy, you swore," Hadley said in a shocked voice.

"I'm sorry, Hadley."

Hugo came around the corner wearing a mismatch of various winter clothing. "I want to go play in the snow."

"No, Hugo," Linc said sternly.

"You're mean."

"Everything okay over there, Linc?" Nadine asked.

What time was too early to start drinking?

"New game plan," he decided suddenly. "We are all going to work," he announced to the twins.

"Yay!"

Hadley decided she had to wear her purple sparkle headband to the office. Only, no one could find the purple sparkle headband. He tried to appease her with various other sparkly hair accessories, but she would have none of it. She stomped her feet, which Linc knew was the precursor to a meltdown.

"Quick, Hugo, search every inch of this house to find your sister's headband."

Hugo nodded wisely. "Got it."

Luckily, they ended up finding the headband in her backpack. However, by that time, she no longer wanted to wear it. Plus, the house now resembled a war zone.

He bundled the kids up, grabbed some coloring books and other toys he thought might keep them entertained, and drove them the short distance to the office. Normally, he liked to walk or bike, but with the snow, he wasn't sure how the kids would do.

They entered the office and a flurry of excitement ensued. Nadine made a big fuss over them. Hats, scarves, and coats flew off.

"Who wants hot chocolate?" Nadine asked.

"With marshmallows?"

"Of course."

Linc knew Nadine was distracting the kids so he could check on the servers. He was so preoccupied fixing the situation he didn't even notice that Mia wasn't at her desk. Nadine kept the kids in the kitchen for about a half hour, just enough time to get everything running smoothly again.

"And we are back up," he said with a final keystroke.

"That's great."

His head shot up at the sound of Mia's voice. "Where did you come from?"

She laughed. "I was making some copies for Nadine when you came in. I thought I would bring you this." She set a steaming cup of coffee in front of him. "Nadine told me how you take yours."

"Thank you," he said gratefully. "Words cannot express how much I need this. I will give you a raise if you added alcohol to it."

She laughed again. "Sorry, looks like I'll to stick to my salary for the time being. But I'll remember that for next time. Rough morning?"

"Am not," Hugo yelled from the kitchen.

"Are too," Hadley countered.

Linc rubbed at his temples. "You don't have kids, do you?" he asked Mia.

"Nope. I just enjoy other peoples for the time being."

"I don't know how much joy you're going to get out of mine, but at least they'll only be here for a couple hours today."

After a very long swallow of piping hot coffee, he took a moment to take in Mia. She was dressed more casually today. She had on a pretty lilac sweater and a pair of jeans that hugged her curves. She had a pair of furry snow boots on her feet. Her cheeks had a light pink tint to them as if she'd just come in from the cold, and her lips were a rosy red. He wanted to snuggle with her by a fire.

"You're pretty," Hadley said to Mia, appearing out of nowhere and mirroring Linc's thoughts. Linc only wished he could be as bold as his daughter. "Daddy, don't you think she's pretty?"

Mia grinned and looked from Hadley up to him.

"Well? Don't you, Daddy?" Hadley never backed down when she wanted an answer. It used to be one of his favorite things about his daughter. He was now reconsidering that.

"I think you're pretty, too," Hugo said. "But I have a girl-friend in nursery school."

Mia let out a small laugh. "Oh really? Who is this girlfriend?"

"Her name is Sophia," Hadley said, twisting back and forth.

Mia raised her brows at Linc, who stifled a groan. "And these would be my children. Hadley, Hugo, this is Ms. Mia."

"Hi, Ms. Mia," they said in unison. To the average person, they had to look like perfect angels.

"Nice to meet you both. Welcome to the office."

"Our power went out," Hadley informed her.

"Really? I bet that was scary."

Hadley nodded. Then she grabbed Mia's hand and held on. "I like your earrings."

"Thank you."

"I like your necklace, too."

Mia ran her fingers over the long necklace. It had a feather at the bottom. "Thank you. I got this in Arizona."

"Where's Arizona?" Hugo asked.

"Come on, I'll show you." Mia walked the kids to her desk and pulled up a map on her computer. She was pointing out where Virginia was. Then she dragged her finger across the map to Arizona. The twins were riveted.

Linc exchanged a look with Nadine, who wore an expression that clearly said, *well, look at that.*

He glanced back and saw that Mia was giving Hadley and Hugo pieces of paper. She was asking them to draw her very specific things and promising to hang their art at her desk.

"You really don't have to entertain them," Linc said, walking over.

"It's no problem. Besides, when Nadine hired me, she said I would be doing all kinds of different things to help out."

"I don't think any of those tasks involved babysitting."

"I really don't mind. And I'm not babysitting. My two new assistants have a very important job."

"Yes, we do, Daddy," Hadley said.

"Ms. Mia needs artwork for her desk because she just started. We are helping her decorate."

"Everything's under control here," Mia said.

"If you're sure," Linc said, completely unsure.

"You and Nadine hired me to help the two of you. Let me help."

With that, Linc nodded and returned to his desk. He waited a full two minutes before he looked back at Mia. When he did, he had to do a double-take.

Hugo was showing Mia what he'd drawn. But Hadley—his little Hadley, who was usually a bit more reserved around women—had climbed up on Mia's lap and was giving her a hug. All three of them were laughing.

Linc stopped breathing for a moment. It felt like someone was squeezing his heart. Even when their mother had been around, Chrissy wasn't a touchy-feely person with the kids. Seeing how peaceful and happy Hugo and Hadley were with Mia was amazing.

And that scared him more than anything else.

***

Mia didn't think entertaining four-year-old twins had been part of the "other duties as assigned" line of her job description. But she had to admit, she'd really enjoyed playing with Hugo and Hadley.

Mia used to get a baby doll every Christmas. She was one of those little girls who adored playing mother; feeding her doll and dressing her up in cute clothes. When she got older, she loved babysitting for the neighborhood kids. Even in college, her sorority sisters always commented on how she would make a great mother and would probably be one of the first to have children.

But when things got serious with Charlie, she'd pushed that desire to mother out of her mind. Maybe it was her subconscious way of knowing her relationship with Charlie wasn't right. And certainly not the ideal situation to introduce a child.

Now…she wasn't sure. Mia chewed on her lip as she considered. Playing with Linc's kids had brought back a lot of feelings she'd assumed were gone. The joy of being around children. Watching how easily excitable they were.

Wasn't she supposed to be thinking about her new life and all of the fun adventures she was going to have this year? Kids didn't lend themselves to being spontaneous and impulsive. As much as she had enjoyed playing with Hadley and Hugo, it was her time to be selfish and enjoy life for once.

Still, she couldn't contain the smile as she remembered the song Hadley was singing. Or, trying to sing. She was getting all the words mixed up, which made both her and Hugo laugh. She glanced at the drawings they had made for her desk. They certainly brightened her workspace.

At their departure, the office became drenched in silence. It was as if all the energy had been sucked from the room. That was probably for the best. Nadine had given her a project that needed her full, undivided attention. It wasn't difficult, but extremely tedious.

Around four, Nadine left for a meeting. Desperately needing a break, Mia went into the kitchen and made herself a coffee. As she was walking back to her desk, she saw Linc leaning close to one of his screens, completely enraptured in something.

She decided he probably needed some caffeine as much as she did. Luckily, she already knew how he took his, so she quickly fixed the coffee and walked over to his workspace.

He jumped when she put the mug down on his desk, knocking over a cup that held about ten different pens. He recovered quickly, smiling at her. "Coffee. Bless you."

"You're welcome," she said, rolling her head in semi-circles.

"Sore neck?" he asked.

"I was bent over my computer going through some spreadsheets for Nadine."

"Need a break?" She nodded, and he pulled a spare chair over. "Let's have coffee together."

She sat down. Linc opened the bottom drawer of his desk and her eyes practically popped out of her head. The entire drawer was jam-packed with food. Chips, cookies, licorice, candy bars, and more.

"Holy junk food, Batman," she said.

He laughed. "Consider yourself a very lucky person. I never reveal this drawer to anyone. It's my personal stash, and it gets me through any kind of possible disaster."

Mia peered closer. "I'm getting a pimple just looking."

"Then you might as well eat something. Take your pick."

She considered for a minute before deciding on a mini Mounds bar. "I love chocolate and coconut."

"Great combo." Linc picked a full-sized Snickers. They enjoyed their chocolate treats in companionable silence.

Linc threw his wrapper into the small trashcan under his desk. "How are you settling in?"

Mia washed down the Mounds with a long sip of coffee. "Great. I mean, it's obviously only been two days, but I think I can do this job well."

"Remind me where you were before this."

52

Mia shifted in the desk chair. She'd liked working at her mom's store, yet she often felt a little embarrassed admitting that was the only place she'd ever worked. "I, um, worked at my mom's bridal boutique."

"That's right," Linc said, completely unphased. "Did you like working with brides on a daily basis?"

She grinned, thinking of all the different personality types she saw at the store. Everything from the dreaded bridezillas to the indecisive bride. Not to mention those women who simply wanted to please everyone else. Throw in some opinionated bridesmaids and an envious friend or two, and it usually made for some interesting days.

"It definitely had its moments. Both good and bad."

Deciding she didn't want to dwell on her prior work experience or lack thereof, she changed the subject. "Can I ask you a question?"

"Sure."

"We went to school together for all those years."

"Since the fifth grade."

"Right, since elementary school." She chewed on her lip for a moment. "Why did you never talk to me?"

Linc emitted a mirthless laugh. "Talk to *the* Amelia Dewitt? Are you kidding?"

"What are you talking about?"

"In case you forgot, you were kind of a big deal."

"No, I wasn't."

"Uh, yes, you were. You were homecoming queen and prom queen."

"That wasn't until our senior year."

"You were also head cheerleader. Plus, you were the most popular girl in our class. Actually, you were the most popular girl in the whole school, no matter what grade we were in."

She shook her head. "That's not true." Was it?

"You were also really bright."

That made her pause.

Linc didn't seem to notice. He continued. "I remember you always did so well in English class. Mr. Damon used to rave about your writing."

Linc's words actually set her heart racing. No one ever really talked about her intelligence. Her looks, sure. Her marriage, absolutely.

She'd done well in English during college too. But it wasn't something her mother asked her about on breaks. Instead, she'd fill her in on what was happening in the sorority or with her boyfriend.

Linc sat forward. "Remember how we used to have to do those integrated group projects?"

She nodded, holding her breath to see what he was going to say about her.

"Those were torture for this introvert." He chucked a thumb toward his chest. "But you were phenomenal standing in front of the class, explaining your group's project. You were the first one in our class to utilize videos and social media."

"I loved putting those presentations together," she said more to herself than him.

"Not to mention all those pageants you used to do. It was so glamorous."

She chuckled. "Glamorous, huh? You've clearly never been to a pageant."

"You'd show your girlfriends all those pictures of you in sequined dresses with your hair all done up. I mean, not that I was looking."

She laughed. "Of course not."

"To sum up," he continued, "You were popular and well-liked and self-assured. And I was not. I was the painfully shy, nerdy kid who used to hide out in the library. You were the beautiful queen of the school."

She opened her mouth, but her words evaporated as she homed in on something he'd just said. "Beautiful?" she whispered.

He nodded. "You still are." His face immediately flushed red.

"Well, thank you."

He fidgeted with his glasses. "I probably shouldn't say things like that to you."

She shrugged. "It's actually nice to hear. It's been a while since a man has complimented me." And no one had ever praised her on her intellect. She still couldn't get over that fact.

Although, she hadn't meant to say anything about her lack of masculine admiration. Sadly, it was true. She hadn't been on any dates since she decided to leave Charlie. Even when she was with her ex, he hadn't been the most romantic of partners.

She knew Charlie thought she was beautiful, but he'd never use that word. He'd express himself in his own way.

You look hot, babe.

Your body is rockin' in that dress.

I have the hottest wife in the firm.

Definitely not poetry. He'd been a bit more sensitive when he'd originally started wooing her. And his compliments, however unpolished they were, didn't bother her. People had different ways of expressing themselves.

"I have to be honest. I'm surprised you're not married," Linc said as if reading her mind and knowing she'd been thinking about her marriage. "You always seemed to have a boyfriend in high school, plus a hundred other guys hanging around you, wishing and hoping you'd break up with the current guy to be with them."

"A hundred guys were following me around?" she said, batting her eyelashes dramatically. "Oh my. I had no idea."

"It was pretty crazy. They had their own lanes in the cafeteria and a separate glee club where they sang your praises."

"Oh, ha ha. Aren't you clever?"

Linc grinned. But the grin faded. "I'm sorry. You *were* married."

She nodded slowly.

"I don't mean to pry, but how long were you married?"

She cast her eyes down. "Only about six months."

Out of the corner of her eye, she saw that he went brows up but stayed quiet.

"Charlie and I weren't right for each other. Marrying him was a mistake."

"I know what you mean."

"You do?"

It was as if he hadn't realized he'd said that out loud. He became thoughtful for a long moment. "Chrissy and I got married the way we did a lot of things, on a whim. One day, she said, 'Hey, let's get married.' So, we did."

"Wow. Did you elope?"

He nodded. "Chrissy was a free spirit. I, as you can probably tell, am not."

She grinned.

"But it was exciting when we first met. I'd been so dedicated to my education. In high school, I was taking college classes instead of drinking cheap beer and flirting with girls at football games. In college, I was determined to learn as much as I could. My friend Alex and I had already started our business too. I graduated in three years. I went to MIT and Chrissy went to Boston College. We met my last year in school. She was a breath of fresh air."

He pushed away from his desk. "It was the first time I felt like I was more than just a computer nerd."

"I happen to think you're way more than a computer nerd. You're more than a laptop, iPad, and smartphone all mixed together."

"That might be the nicest thing anyone has ever said to me. See, that's why you were so popular in school. You were beautiful and kind."

"There's that beautiful word again."

Just like the first time he'd called her beautiful, Linc blushed. God, he was so adorable. And he asked her questions and actually seemed interested in her answers. She could never get Charlie off his cell long enough to have a decent conversation.

Linc was no Charlie. Thank goodness. Linc was...the kind of man she should have ended up with.

She sighed loudly.

"Are you okay?" Linc asked.

"Yes. I'm being…regretful," she decided.

"That's never a good thing. Trust me. I've been down the road of regrets, and it leads to nowhere."

"You sound wise, Linc McMann."

"I have my moments."

"Yes, you do."

Somehow, they'd moved their chairs closer. When had that happened? When they were discussing regrets or when he was calling her beautiful?

Linc nailed her with a gaze that was both kind and, if she wasn't mistaken, lustful. Behind those glasses, he had the prettiest light brown eyes. They were caring, and she knew that if she let herself, she could get lost in them.

She let out an exhale. She couldn't let herself get lost. In fact, she needed to ground herself immediately.

It hadn't been that long ago when she'd allowed herself to get wrapped up with her ex-husband. In the beginning, things with Charlie had been exciting and romantic. Look how that turned out in the end.

The stakes were even higher now. She worked with Linc. He owned the company that was giving her a new life and fresh start. Throw in those two adorable kids and the recipe becomes even more complicated. It wasn't just Linc. It was Linc and his family. She obviously didn't know the whole story, but from what he'd revealed already, he'd been through the wringer with his ex. Especially if he'd been on regret road.

She also chastised herself for her reaction to being called beautiful. Mia couldn't deny that having someone who thought she was pretty and had admired her in high school inflated her ego. Disgusted with the thought, she had to clamp down on a groan. If the last ten years—or, hell, even longer—had taught her anything, wasn't it that beauty was fleeting? Perfection was tiring. Doing everything exactly right did not lead to fulfillment.

The door flew open and Mia pushed her chair back from Linc's desk. Nadine entered the office along with a cold burst of wind. Just what she needed.

"How's it going in here?" Nadine asked, oblivious to what had almost just transpired.

"Great," Linc said.

"Fine, she uttered.

Linc stood, knocking his coffee cup over in the process. Luckily there was only a small amount of liquid left, but it quickly began trailing over the desk. Mia grabbed some tissues and helped him dab up the mess. Then she fled back to the safety of her workspace.

When she'd decided to take time to find herself and live, it had definitely not included making stupid decisions.

And allowing herself to feel anything for Linc, no matter how small, was definitely a stupid decision.

Chapter Four

A new week, a new Mia.

Over the weekend, she'd taken stock of her first week at work. Not to mention her crushing on Linc, or her...whatever the heck it was. She'd absolutely preened at the idea of someone thinking she was more than a doll to be arranged however they wanted. Sure, Linc said she was beautiful, but he'd also said she was bright. Even now, that idea gave her little butterflies.

Still, she was a grown-up and she needed to start acting like one. She needed to take back control of her job, her life...her hormones.

If reining in all those things meant she had to keep a safe—er, professional—distance from Linc—a hard feat in their small office space—well, then, she'd do it.

Mia threw herself into her work during the day. She was trying to learn all the non-IT aspects of Something True. She was making lists and organizing files. She'd cleaned up their shared drive, creating folders for each action item. Nadine had even complimented her multiple times on her organizational skills.

On her personal computer drive though, she was making other lists. Ideas for the website. She'd even found a contest she thought they should enter. It would give the site invaluable attention.

After five o'clock, Mia was enjoying being a carefree, single girl for the first time in her life. Back when she worked at the bridal boutique, she usually didn't close until nine. Plus, they were always open on the weekends. That meant she didn't get to socialize during normal socializing times. Being able to go to happy hours now was a revelation. And she'd already been to quite a few. She'd also gone to meet-ups and parties.

Mia started trying new restaurants and coffee shops. Her sister suggested she join one of the online dating sites. Surprisingly, she considered it for a hot second. While it hadn't been that long since the end of her marriage, the relationship had been over long before that. They'd been going through the motions. But was she really ready to be someone's doll again? Was it too soon?

Hating even thinking about it, she turned her attention toward her ultimate goal, the sign of her really being her own independent person. She was going to go skydiving. That's right, Mia Reynolds was going to go up in a plane and jump back to Earth. She'd heard from so many people that skydiving was the ultimate rush. A group of her sorority sisters had done it back in college, but her boyfriend hadn't wanted her to join them. So, she didn't. But now, there was no boyfriend to stop her. She'd have to wait for the weather to get better, but she'd found a reputable skydiving company and was following their social media daily.

She couldn't be prouder of herself.

Yet, as she entered invoices for Nadine, she couldn't stop looking over at Linc. He was just so damn cute. She shouldn't be attracted to him. Linc wasn't her type. Not the way his glasses were sliding down his nose and the fact that he had some big food stain on his shirt and a missing button on his sleeve.

He was currently crouched over his main computer screen, typing ferociously. His typical pose, she'd learned. Any minute now, his phone would ring. The twins liked to call him around this time of day to say hi and tell him about everything they'd been doing.

Right on time, his phone rang. Mia smiled as he picked it up and greeted Hugo. She went back to invoice processing. Not the most interesting task on the planet, but she enjoyed the busy work.

Her cell phone vibrated, and she turned it over. She saw a message from her friend, Karen, apologizing profusely. She wouldn't be able to make it to the escape room Mia had booked for tonight. Unfortunately, she'd already paid for it and it was too late to cancel.

She could still go, but what fun would it be to do an escape room by herself? She quickly called a couple different people to see if they could take Karen's place. One by one, no one was free on a Friday night with two hours warning. Shocker.

"No, Grace, I totally understand," she was saying to her roommate. She'd already known that Grace had plans to go to dinner at her fiancé's parents' house. She was just checking in case Grace's plans had fallen through. It was her last-ditch effort.

Mia laughed mirthlessly as she listened to Grace's groan on the other end of the phone. "I know, you'd much rather go to an escape room than hang out with Xander's parents. No, don't worry about it." She hung up the phone and let out a big sigh.

"Everything okay?"

She jumped, not having realized that Linc was standing at her desk. "Yes, no. It's not that big of a deal."

"You sounded pretty disappointed on the phone. Sorry, I didn't mean to eavesdrop." He handed her an invoice and then leaned on the wall of her cubicle, shaking the wall and causing the small potted plant she'd brought in to jiggle dangerously.

Mia steadied the plant. "That's okay. It's a small office." She told him how her friend wasn't able to make the escape room she'd already booked.

"Maybe…maybe I can come with you."

She had to work hard to keep her mouth from falling open. "Seriously? What about the twins?"

"Actually, Hadley and Hugo have a big night planned."

"Oh really? Are they going out on the town?"

He grinned his lopsided smile. A smile she'd really started to dig. "Well, the four-year-old equivalent of a night out on the town. It's their friend Oliver's birthday. Oliver's parents are taking a bunch of them to see that new animated movie and then back to their house for a pizza party. Oliver's parents are brave people."

"That sounds fun. I'm sure they'll love it."

"Yeah. But it means that I am a free man for a couple of hours."

"My reservation is at six. That should give you plenty of time to get back to the kids."

"In that case, I would love to go." He ran a hand through his hair. "Just one question. What's an escape room?"

She laughed. "Oh, it's really fun, and actually, you'd probably be really good at it. Escape rooms are these puzzles where you go in and have to figure out different clues in order to get out of the room. There's a time limit."

"What happens if you don't get out of the room in time?"

She let her smile fade, and she leaned toward him shaking her head slowly. "It's bad," she whispered.

"Really?"

Mia kept the same serious tone as she said, "No." Then she laughed. She couldn't help it.

"You're teasing me?"

Playfully, she punched his shoulder. "You're too easy."

"Something that was never said about me in high school," he said with a big grin.

"Nothing happens. You just don't win. But trust me, once you get in there and your adrenaline is going, you want to solve the puzzle." She shuffled her feet. "Sooo, you still wanna come with me?"

He paused, studying her for a few moments. Mia's mind raced. Would he want to go with her? Should he go with her? She was supposed to be keeping her distance from him. Yet, the idea of spending time with Linc outside of the office suddenly seemed extra appealing.

Linc was levelheaded though. He always had been. Surely, he would realize they should just say good night, and each leave the office. Separately.

"I would love to."

There went that.

***

Not only did they solve all of the clues and get out of the escape room, but they did it in record time. Linc took a lot of satisfaction in seeing their team name—The Reunited Alums—written in the number one spot on the record board.

He may have had no idea what an escape room was earlier, but now he was all about it. This was right up his alley. Mia was right. Once he'd gotten in there, his adrenaline peaked, and he was all in. Those clues didn't stand a chance.

Because they'd finished so quickly, Linc still had time to spare before picking up the twins. While he knew there was a mountain of laundry waiting for him at home, somehow, he wasn't quite feeling it. Or, maybe that had more to do with the fact that Mia had changed into a pair of tight-fitting jeans and a black top that had sequins around the neckline. She looked chic and beautiful, and quite frankly, she could have asked him to jump off the Woodrow Wilson Bridge and he would have done it. Before he realized what he was doing, his mouth was moving and he was inviting her out for a post-escape room celebratory drink.

Now, they were sitting at the bar in a trendy Spanish tapas restaurant, enjoying a sweet red wine sangria and sharing three different dishes. And, of course, they were relishing in their escape room victory.

"I've only been to an escape room one other time, but we definitely killed it," Mia said.

Linc raised his glass to toast, but instead, some of the red liquid sloshed over the edge. Mia laughed and helped him wipe it up. Linc inwardly cringed. He would never be the suave, debonair type. At least, Mia didn't seem to mind. She wore a big smile on her face as she sat back and attempted a toast again.

"To the best escape room winners of all time." She touched her glass against his gingerly.

Linc enjoyed seeing her all smiles and confidence now. "Cheers," he said, pushing his glasses back up his nose, before deciding to remove them altogether. They were really just for reading and computer use anyway.

She sipped her drink and then snagged a piece of cheese from one of their plates. "Any word from Hadley and Hugo?"

Linc turned his phone over to find a blank screen. "Nope. Which is a good thing. Trust me. If there was a problem, I would know."

"They're probably having so much fun."

He appreciated that she asked about his kids. That she thought of them at all meant the world to him. In the two years since his divorce, he'd been on a whopping total of three dates. Two were setups and one was his very brief foray into online dating. None went past the first date. All had been disastrous, reminding him that he didn't want to get involved with anyone ever again.

Even though he'd been very upfront about his children and home situation, not one of those dates asked him about Hadley and Hugo. But Mia did.

Mia also had his children's artwork hanging in her cubicle. Now that he thought about it, she asked about them daily.

The feeling was mutual too because both of the twins talked about Mia. Especially Hadley, who sang Mia's praises daily. Those few hours together had certainly made an indelible impression on his little princess. He could only imagine if they'd spent even more time together.

Mia shifted on her barstool. "You know, there was a moment back at the office when I thought you weren't going to come tonight. You had paused for a long time."

He knew exactly the moment she was referring to. Although his intentions were always to go with her, he'd been caught by something. Something that took him aback. Something that wasn't congruous with the Amelia Dewitt he knew back in high school.

"I did," he said slowly. He waited while the bartender refilled their glasses of sangria. "I was thinking about high school."

"Okay," she said in an uncertain tone.

"I know, it doesn't seem related. But go with me on this one."

"Okay," she repeated, a little more confident this time.

She put the straw to her lips and took a sip of her sangria. Linc's gaze was drawn to her mouth. That mouth that was painted a soft pink. A mouth that he used to study endlessly back in high school.

"Linc?" she asked, pulling him out of his thoughts.

67

"Sorry." He tasted his sangria to give him a moment to collect himself. The sweet flavor of the drink coated his suddenly dry throat.

"I was thinking about you back in high school. You were so…" He trailed off as he searched for the right word. "Dynamic."

She grinned at that.

"You were confident, without being cocky or conceited, although you could have been either. You were so pretty and perfect."

He couldn't miss that her smile faded at the word perfect.

She clutched her necklace; a delicate silver necklace with a circle pendant that had an A for Amelia inscribed on it. He'd noticed she wore it every day. For a moment, she stared off into the distance.

"That was me, perfect Amelia."

Interesting. "Most kids wanted to be you. They were trying every day to be perfect versions of themselves."

She winced. "Perfection is exhausting."

He wasn't sure what to say to that. "Well, like I said, you were so confident back then. Earlier today, I saw a different side to you. You seemed unsure and…shy. In fact, since you've started working with us, you seem very different than the Amelia I remember."

She expelled a long breath. "I wish I could say that people change over the years, because, of course, they do. But that's not really the case with me. I guess I'm going through something." She tilted her head, considering. "I'm going through a transformation."

"From Amelia to Mia?" he asked.

"Kind of, yeah. My divorce really woke me up."

He nodded. He'd been there. His own divorce hadn't simply been the end of a marriage. Linc considered it the defining line of maturity in his life.

"Want to talk about it?" he asked, then immediately regretted it. He knew better than anyone how personal and debilitating ending a marriage could be. He didn't like talking about his own situation. "Sorry," he said, touching Mia's hand. "I shouldn't have asked."

She shook her head and shrugged. Her body language was casual, but her light blue eyes had darkened. They spoke volumes.

Mia was quiet for a long time. He figured she didn't want to talk about it. Finally, she turned to him.

"When I decided to end my marriage—my six-month-long marriage—everything changed for me. It wasn't just that my marriage was wrong. Even though, it was a complete disaster. But, it was so much more. Looking back, I see that most of my life was wrong too."

Interested, Linc leaned forward. "What do you mean? You always seemed to have such a great life."

"Please don't get me wrong. I had a lot of wonderful things in my life. But…but, I wasn't really living." She shook her head again. "I'm not making sense."

Linc remained silent, allowing her time to gather her thoughts.

"I always did everything that was expected of me. Everything. I was the perfect daughter." She scrunched up her nose. "Perfect. I really hate that word."

"It's a tough word," Linc said. "Nothing can live up to it."

"Exactly," she said with a very long sigh.

She took a long pull of her sangria. "I did everything my parents wanted me to do. I was a pageant girl and a cheerleader. I went to the college they wanted me to go to."

"You went to…Clemson, right?" He remembered. "Did you not like it?"

"No, that's not…" She squirmed in her seat. "I did like it. But it wasn't really my choice to go there."

"Where did you want to go?"

"That's just it." She threw up her hands. "I didn't even have ideas of where I wanted to go to college. Both my parents went to Clemson, so I was going to go there too. I pledged the same sorority as my mother."

Trying to find the bright side, Linc pointed. "You were in a sorority. That must have been fun."

"It was okay. I guess. I don't know. Because of my birthday, I'm too young for my class. That meant I didn't turn twenty-one until well into my senior year. I was often the sober sister, who had to stay up late and pick up my friends from the party where they were having fun."

She pushed some food around on one of the plates but didn't eat any. "I dated a guy in college too. We met at the beginning of freshmen year. So, I never really got to do the dating and hooking up that so many of my friends did."

"You felt like you missed out on some things," Linc guessed.

Her eyes lit up. "Yes. Exactly. It wasn't that I didn't have any fun or didn't like Clemson or Kappa or my life. It's that I missed out on a lot because I was so busy trying to be perfect and fit the mold that other people set for me, that I never experienced anything for myself. To be honest, I never even thought about what I wanted for myself. I just kind of floated along."

"What about your marriage? How does that fit in?"

She groaned. Linc knew she was hurting, but even with her face in a grimace, she looked so freaking adorable.

"After college, I wanted to travel. I had wanted to study abroad while I was in college, but my boyfriend convinced me that he needed me by his side as he vied to become president of his fraternity. So, I didn't leave South Carolina.

"After graduation, I came back here. My plan was to work in my mother's bridal shop for the summer, save up some money, and then take off for Paris." Her shoulders lifted and then fell. "I never went to Paris. I never went anywhere. Until January 2 when I started working at Something True, I continued working for my mother."

"How did you meet your husband?"

"Charlie worked at my dad's law firm. Again, perfection on paper. He had all the right degrees and breeding. In the beginning, he was romantic. He wined and dined me. But as our relationship grew, Charlie became more and more absent. It felt like I was just some accessory that he would bring out at the right moments."

He couldn't ask her, but Linc wondered if she'd even loved this guy. As if reading his mind, Mia spoke up.

"If you're dating someone for a long period of time, you must be in love with them. Why else would you be with them? At least, that's what I told myself. After about a year or so, I started saying I love you. I didn't mean it. But I didn't know that I didn't mean it." She laughed. "Does that make sense?"

"Maybe you just wanted to be in love?"

"I definitely did."

"Six months into my marriage, my sister met her husband, Jack. I saw the way Em and Jack looked at each other, the way they were around each other. I was jealous, so insanely jealous. I realized I wanted that kind of passion too. I wanted more than Charlie."

"You filed for divorce," Linc said.

"Not only that. It was like everything became clear to me. I hadn't really lived yet. At least, I hadn't lived the life I wanted. Not that there's anything wrong with Mama's store, but that was the only place I'd ever worked."

"You wanted more." He repeated her words.

She slapped her hand on top of his. "Yes. I went from my parent's house to the sorority house back to my parents' house to my husband."

"You never lived in your own place?"

She shook her head. "Never. And I realized I craved that. Even to have roommates and be mad that someone doesn't do the dishes. Or take out the trash. Or eats my ice cream and doesn't replace it." She laughed. "It might seem ridiculous but there are so many little things I never experienced."

"What about friends?" he asked.

"I have some, but because of the hours I used to work, and then dating Charlie so young, I didn't put much effort into it. I wanted to go to happy hours and parties. I wanted to…I don't know."

"What?" he asked, curious.

"Go to a kegger."

Linc chuckled. "And drink out of a red solo cup?"

"Yes, totally. I want to go to the movies by myself and buy clothes that are totally impractical. I want to buy shoes that aren't for work and aren't for exercising. Shoes that are impractical and decadent and just for me."

Linc was getting the full picture now. Not only did his heart go out to her, but he was understanding why she'd gone from the perfect Amelia he remembered from high school to this version of herself. Mia was a work in progress who desperately needed to try new things and make up for a lifetime of toeing the line.

"You understand?" She asked this question in such a tiny, quiet voice that Linc almost missed it. Her eyes widened, and he could tell that she was dead serious.

"Yes, I do. You need a chance to live life."

She exhaled a huge breath and then smiled. "I need a chance to figure out what kind of life I want to live."

"You deserve that chance, Mia."

"Thank you." She placed her hand over his.

Even though her touch was light, it was setting off a very potent reaction in his body. A reaction that felt wonderful yet terrified him at the same time.

"There are so many things I want to do."

"Besides drinking crappy beer out of a solo cup?" he asked.

She grinned. "Besides that."

"What else?"

"I've always wanted to take a salsa lesson."

73

"Like how to make salsa?"

She burst out laughing. "No, silly. Salsa dancing." She kept laughing for the next few moments. "I want to take weekend trips."

"Anywhere in particular?"

"I'm not sure yet. Maybe New York to see a show, or down to the Outer Banks. Maybe even Atlantic City."

"Do you like to gamble?" Linc asked.

She threw her hands up again. "I don't know. I've never done that before either."

She leaned forward as if she was going to tell him the secrets to every mystery in the world. "Something that I really, really want to do is jump out of a plane."

Linc leaned forward too. "Are you serious?"

"Totally."

"Um, that's terrifying."

"But I bet it's exhilarating too."

Linc liked seeing the color return to her face. She was flush with excitement and it made her that much more attractive to him. Her eyes sparkled and her skin glowed. This was the girl he remembered.

And just like that, it was as if Linc was back in tenth-grade English, watching her from the back of the room. All of those feelings of attraction came racing back. He remembered how he would fantasize about her. If he could just be her boyfriend, then everything in his life would go right.

Perfection. She'd talked about it. And now that he was older and wiser, he knew perfection was seldom perfect. He'd never really sought it out anyway. Give him a messy kitchen, his two frazzled kids, and a missing shirt button any day.

Still, Linc was drawn to her. The way she was so comfortable around him. The way she could talk without seeming awkward. He was enthralled watching her sip her sangria.

"Tonight has been amazing, Linc."

Mia was in such a transitionary state. He shouldn't complicate matters for her. Still, he literally couldn't glance in her direction without his brain screaming, *kiss her!* Mia might have regrets about a lot of things in her life, but Linc's biggest regret was never working up the courage to kiss her.

He blew out a breath of frustration. What was he thinking? He hadn't wanted to kiss a woman in forever. And Mia wasn't just a woman. She was someone he'd known for a long time who was currently working for him.

"I've really enjoyed this time with you," he told her.

Kiss her. Kiss her. Kiss her.

He'd never been great at interpreting signs from the opposite sex, but he was pretty sure they'd connected tonight. Maybe she was feeling the same pull as he was.

She leaned toward him and placed a hand against his arm. His skin burned where she touched him. Her gaze moved over him, seemingly taking him in. He did the same, zeroing in on her mouth.

Her lips moved, and she whispered, "It's really great to have you as a friend."

The "f" word.

Clearly, Linc's streak of not understanding women continued. A completely different "f" word popped into his mind as he sat back and tried to be friends for the rest of the evening.

Chapter Five

Mia had a new friend. They hadn't done anything together outside of work since the escape room, but she and Linc had quickly formed a camaraderie in the office.

They ate lunch together every day. Sometimes he would buy her a sandwich or salad from one of the local restaurants. Other times, she would make something at home and bring it in for him. Since Mia was just learning how to cook, there was a fifty-fifty chance her lunches were edible.

Today, Linc took a bite of the tuna salad she'd made. He tried to smile, but the rest of his face squished together. "This is, um, great."

She laughed. "Liar."

"No really. It's good."

"Linc, your face is turning green." She took the sandwich from him.

She threw both her sandwich and his directly in the trash. "I swear I followed the recipe."

He laughed. "I believe you."

She exhaled a frustrated breath. "What kind of idiot can't make tuna salad?"

Linc turned sympathetic eyes in her direction. "You can't win 'em all. Besides, you made that really good pasta last week. Try the tuna fish again. I bet you can make it better next time."

She couldn't stop the smile from spreading. No matter what she was doing, Linc supported her. The other day she was having a heck of a time with a computer program they were using. Patiently, he went over the program with her, never failing in his estimation that she would get it. She loved that someone was encouraging her. Ultimately, she did get the program and continued to use it every day.

"Fine, I'll give it another try this weekend. What are we going to do for lunch now?" she asked, her stomach grumbling in protest.

He considered. "How about a pizza? Nadine, you want in if we order pizza?"

"Wish I could," Nadine called from across the room. "But I have a lunch date with a friend. You two enjoy." She stood, gathering her purse and coat.

"What do you say?" he asked.

"You can never go wrong with pizza."

"Unless you make it," Linc teased.

"Shut up. I'm trying."

"You know I'm not being serious. But since you've taken an active interest in cooking, maybe you should add cooking

78

classes to your long list of activities. There are a ton of places around here that offer them."

Not a bad idea.

An hour later, the remnants of their pizza lunch were spread over the table in the kitchen. They'd both brought their laptops in while they ate. Mia was keeping an eye on the site's inbox. She could also answer the main phone through her computer.

"You know, you are allowed to take a lunch break. The phone can go to voicemail," Linc said with a wry smile.

"I know, but I've noticed we've been getting more calls since you installed that new update and I hate to return to twenty missed calls after enjoying the bliss of this pizza."

However, she wasn't only monitoring things for the website while they ate. Mia took a sip of her Diet Coke and considered. Should she run her ideas by Linc? What would he think?

"I feel like there's a lot happening in there right now." Linc tapped a finger to her forehead.

"Well, I am more than a pretty face," she said, trying to keep it light.

"You are that. What's going on?"

"Well…" Maybe she should talk to Nadine first. Or would it be better to call a meeting and speak with both of them? She would like to get his opinion though.

He pushed his plate to the middle of the table. "Mia?"

"So, I have some ideas." He waited patiently. "About the website. And about the company in general."

"Yeah?" He sat back in his chair and put his glasses back on. "Let's hear it."

"I mean, I'm not trying to overstep my boundaries."

"Mia, you work here. There are only three of us. We value your opinion. You wouldn't be here if we didn't."

She almost gasped at his statement. When was the last time someone valued what she had to say?

She coughed. "Well, I've told you that we used your website a lot at the store. I have some really easy tweaks that would help it be more functional for the average user." She went through her list of adding links to certain areas and combining other pages. She showed him on her laptop one of the sections that didn't fit in with the rest.

"I've noticed this page gets the lowest views of the whole website, both total and unique."

His brows went up. "Have you been looking on the backend?"

"Um, yeah. Remember, you showed me how to see the views on the different pages."

He worked his mouth back and forth. "I did, but that was really quick. I'm impressed you remembered how to do it. Most people don't catch on so quickly."

"It's pretty easy," she said.

"Seriously, Mia, that's impressive."

His words set off those butterflies again. She bit her lip. His encouragement gave her the resolve to keep going.

"Also, I've noticed that our social media is kinda…lacking."

Linc ran a hand through his hair, making some of the strands stick straight up. Mia stifled a giggle. Despite the hairstyle, or maybe because of it, he looked really cute.

He frowned. "Nadine and I discussed how important that is. We've wanted to do more with social media, but we need to get someone in here to do that."

She coughed again. "Maybe I could take a whack at it?" She felt her eyes go wide as she waited for his answer.

"Seriously? Do you have experience with social media? I mean, besides personal use."

She nodded. "I did all the Facebook, Instagram, Pinterest, and Twitter for my mom's store. The last year I was even attending social media and marketing conferences and seminars. It evolves so quickly, you really have to stay on top of trends and know where your customers are visiting."

He studied her for a long time. Mia squirmed in her chair. Maybe she shouldn't have brought it up.

"Mia," he said slowly, obviously still considering. "I think it's a really amazing idea. I would love to see what you could do."

Mia had to work hard to keep her mouth from falling open. "You do? Seriously?"

"Yeah. I mean, we should run it by Nadine too. But I know she would love to have someone doing our social media. Go for it."

Ohmigod. Ohmigod. Ohmigod. "You won't regret it. I'm going to knock it out of the park."

"I have no doubt."

He did? That belief was so heartening to her. No one ever thought of her the way Linc did.

"Now, I found something for you," Linc said, turning his laptop toward her.

Mia scanned the screen and saw he was on Groupon. "What's this?"

"I found a local Groupon that is offering salsa dance lessons. Didn't you say you wanted to take a class?"

She loved that he remembered. "I did. I can't believe you remembered that." She read through the Groupon, getting more excited as she took it in. Until she reached the fine print. She frowned.

"What's wrong?"

"Nothing. It's just that this Groupon is for two people. You have to have a partner to attend the class." She sighed. Quickly, she ran through her personal list of friends. Maybe she could ask one of the guys from her mom's store to go with her.

Linc made a move to push the pizza box further across the table. Somehow, he ended up flipping the box, scattering crumbs and uneaten crusts, and knocking paper plates onto the floor.

Mia laughed. "You know, you have a real talent for being clumsy. I don't even know how you just made that happen." She gestured to the mess.

Linc's cheeks filled with red, and he offered her a contrite smile. "My parents always said I could win the gold medal in clumsiness."

Mia began cleaning up. "I don't know about that. I think you may be more silver or bronze level."

Linc grabbed the plates from the floor. "Would it be humiliating for you to salsa dance with the silver medalist?"

She paused. "What?"

"I don't want to embarrass you or anything. But I'll definitely give it my all."

Was he saying what she thought he was saying? "Linc." She drew out his name slowly. "Are you offering to be my partner at salsa lessons?"

"I mean, I hope that's okay because I kinda already bought the Groupon."

She couldn't stop the grin from spreading. She jumped up. "Linc, thank you so much!" She launched herself at him, wrapping her arms around him in a tight hug.

But what she'd meant to be a fast hug of gratitude quickly turned into something…else. Something more. Linc's arms came around her and his laughter receded.

He smelled good. He felt even better. Linc may be the clumsiest person she knew, but he gave the best hugs. In his arms, Mia felt secure and safe.

She pushed away and bit her lip. She gave a half-laugh, trying to lighten the moment that had somehow turned heady.

"Thank you again, Linc."

He nodded. "I guess we should get used to being close like that. I mean, uh, for the dance lesson."

Mia gulped. She didn't think she'd ever get used to being held by Linc. Even though she wanted his arms around her more than she should.

***

Linc felt one hundred percent certain that he could add something new to his resume. Owner of Something True and CEO of two left feet.

To put it mildly, he was awful at salsa dancing.

But to be fair to all of the other dances, he was probably bad at them too.

"You're doing great, Linc," Mia said breathlessly as they attempted to move around the floor.

It was as if she'd read his mind. While he appreciated the support, he knew he was doing far, far from great.

Mia grimaced, just as Linc stepped on her foot. For the thousandth time. He was sure her feet were probably the width of pancakes now.

The only thing going well was spending more time with Mia. Especially outside of the office. Plus, as much as he loved them, Linc had to admit that he'd really, really needed a night away from the kids.

Of course, that didn't help the usual guilt from settling in quickly when he'd decided to go dancing. Joley picked the twins up after their movie and party with their friends. He knew Hadley and Hugo felt secure with her. In fact, they were probably having even more fun than if he were there.

Still, he would miss bath time, reading a story, and tucking them in. His conscience continued to shame him.

"Remember, look at your partner, not at your feet," their instructor, Debbie, called out.

How was he supposed to get his feet to move the right way when he couldn't look at them? Begrudgingly, his eyes flicked up to meet Mia's amused gaze.

Bad move. He would never be able to concentrate on his feet—or anything else—when he was staring at the gorgeous woman before him. The gorgeous woman with the big, dazzling smile.

Mia had shown up in a short-sleeved red dress. No, not red exactly. A scarlet dress, he decided. The top of the dress kind of tied around her, hugging her curves, while the bottom flared out, twisting around her long legs as she moved across the floor. Her hair was pulled back into a loose ponytail, with strands falling down to frame her pretty face. She'd added a rose behind one ear. "For dramatic effect," she'd told him. It only helped to highlight the red she'd painted on her lips.

When she'd first walked into the dance studio, his mouth had practically watered. She'd been all smiles; so excited to finally take this salsa lesson. Happiness exuded from her. She was the most beautiful woman he'd ever seen.

Unlike when they were in high school and his libido told him that Mia was hot and therefore he should lust after her, things were different now. They were adults. And they'd been getting to know each other. Each day, Linc discovered that he liked more and more of Mia. She was funny and smart. Smarter than she gave herself credit for.

And she was kind. She asked about the kids all the time. Even tonight, she wanted to know if they were okay and who was watching them.

His heart was softening, and that idea terrified him.

"Ouch." Mia grimaced as Linc stepped on her toe.

Again.

"I swear I'll pay for any required foot surgery," he said.

"It's okay," she quickly said. "Don't worry. Just relax and keep going."

"You are way too nice to me," he said.

"You are the one who is nice. I wouldn't even be here if it wasn't for you. And I'm really enjoying this time together."

"No, hold her tighter," Debbie said, shutting off the music. "Dancing is about feeling, emotion. It is about passion. You must exude the passion you feel for your partner. Now, hold Mia like this."

She demonstrated by positioning Linc's arms around Mia. She walked around the two of them with an eagle eye, murmuring incoherent sounds. Before Linc realized what was happening, Debbie pushed him toward Mia.

"There. That is better." She positioned herself right behind Mia's head, which was a good thing because Mia was currently trying not to laugh.

"Now, look deeply into her eyes. Convey your passion."

"Uhhh…" Linc stuttered.

Debbie moved, and the music started again. Linc finally looked at Mia. Really looked at her. She was smiling, which lit up her entire face. Her blue eyes twinkled and her cheeks were rosy.

Then his eyes drifted down to her lips. Those enticing, tempting lips.

It would be so easy to convey the passion Debbie wanted. Not only was Mia gorgeous, but they had a history. And more than any of that, she'd grown into a kind, caring woman. A woman who was slowly melting his frozen heart.

"Now, dance," Debbie said sternly.

They began to move together. Linc knew he was the one who was supposed to lead, but he felt more like Mia was the one in control.

Fine by him. At this moment, he felt like he would follow her anywhere.

And that's when he got tripped up. Both literally and figuratively.

He'd followed his ex-wife. He'd allowed himself to go along with her ideas and plans. He'd married on a whim. Where had that taken him? Loving a woman the way he did Chrissy led him to be far more spontaneous and capricious than he truly was. That's how he ended up in divorce court. As a single father.

Back on the dancefloor, his feet were going in every which direction. He was supposed to be going to the left but somehow went to the right. He heard a pop, felt a pain, and the next thing he knew, Linc was on the floor.

It was a bad, bad thing when your body went in one direction and your foot went in a completely opposite direction. Even worse when your heart nudged you in one place when your brain screamed *no, no, no.*

***

Mia couldn't believe they'd somehow gone from dance room to emergency room. Yet, here she was in the hospital in the red dancing dress she'd rush-ordered from Amazon. At least Linc didn't have to wear a hospital gown.

"What's the damage, doc?" Linc asked.

Mia knew Linc was trying to come across as brave. But she could tell he was in pain. When she'd seen his right foot going in the opposite direction, she'd instantly known it wasn't going to end well. His fall to the floor had happened in slow motion.

Somewhere in her mind, she was well aware that Linc had volunteered to go dancing. Heck, he'd even bought the Groupon for the class.

But no reasoning could stop the guilt. She was the one who brought up the salsa class. She was the one who just *had* to try it. This was one hundred percent her fault.

"We have a grade one sprained ankle," Doctor Weber said.

"Is grade one good or bad?" Mia asked, wringing her hands together.

"No sprained ankle is good. But in Linc's case, it shouldn't be too bad. You need to stay off of it for about five to fourteen days."

"Fourteen days?" Linc dropped his head.

"That's worst case. You're young, you're relatively healthy. I'm sure you'll be up and salsa dancing again much quicker."

"I'm not too sure about the salsa dancing."

Mia felt awful. *All your fault. All your fault.*

"Do you know about R.I.C.E.?" the doctor asked.

Mia jumped in. "Rest, ice, compression, elevation," she recited. "My sister was clumsy in our earlier days," she explained.

Doctor Weber nodded. "Your wife has it down."

"Oh, she's not my...," Linc began.

"No, we're not married," Mia finished.

"Sorry," Doctor Weber said. "Well, your girlfriend seems competent and more than able to take care of you.

Girlfriend? Mia noticed that Linc didn't correct the doctor this time. Then again, neither did she.

"Rest – you'll want to stay off that foot for a couple days at least," the doctor said. He began to explain the treatment of a sprained ankle to Linc. "Use ice to keep the swelling down. Over the counter drugs like Ibuprofen will help with inflammation."

"Compression?" Linc asked.

"You'll want to keep that ankle wrapped. The nurse will show you how before you leave here. And make sure to keep the foot elevated as much as possible, but especially when you sleep. Are you a back sleeper?"

Linc shook his head. "I'm all about sprawling on my stomach."

"For the next week or so, you are going to be all about looking up at the ceiling."

The doctor continued talking to Linc, but now all Mia could think about was how Linc slept. She wondered what his bedroom was like. What color was his comforter? Did he read before bed? Maybe he played games on his phone. Did he wear pajamas?

Or nothing at all?

She gulped.

"And the nurse will be in momentarily to wrap that ankle." With that, the doctor left the room.

Linc and Mia were silent for a long moment. "At least, it's only a sprained ankle. It could have been a lot worse," he finally said.

"True," she said. Mia took the seat next to the bed that the doctor had vacated. "I'm really sorry, Linc."

He turned surprised eyes in her direction. "What on Earth are you sorry for?"

"Taking you salsa dancing. If I hadn't—"

"I wouldn't have had as much fun as I had tonight," he finished.

"But, but…" She stammered. "You wouldn't have gotten injured either.

"That was an accident, Mia. Really. There is no need for you to take the blame for my clumsiness."

She sighed and blew out a long breath of air. "I suppose you're right."

"Of course, I'm right." He offered a big smile.

"I hope you don't have anything coming up for the next week or so. Any rugby games, dance-offs, marathons?"

Linc chuckled. "Nope, I had my last dance-off just the other day." He reached down and adjusted the ice pack the doctor had placed on his foot. "Luckily, I can work from home. Oh shoot," he said, sitting up straight.

"What?" Mia leapt off the chair, ready to help with any pain.

"This is my right foot. I won't be able to drive."

Mia relaxed slightly.

"I can work from home, but the kids. I'm going to have to figure out something for Hadley and Hugo. I need to get them to and from school." Linc dropped back against the pillows. "I don't even want to think about the stairs. Going up and down is going to be tough."

Once again, Mia felt awful. She'd injured a single parent with not one, but two, active four-year-olds relying on him. "It must be really hard parenting by yourself." She sat back down quickly. She hadn't actually meant to say that out loud. But now that it was out there, she waited for his response.

"It is hard. It's definitely rewarding too. But yeah, overall, I would love to have someone to not only help out with the difficult things like discipline and cleaning and those really fun days when the stomach flu passes through my house. But it would also be nice to have someone to share the good times with too."

"That makes sense."

"Hugo took his good old time talking. His doctor said it may have been the divorce, or he simply wasn't ready to speak. But when he finally did start talking, I was so excited. I followed him around for days recording every single word he said. Of course, I shared it with my parents and Nadine and some of my friends. Everyone was happy, but it just wasn't, well…you know."

"It wasn't the same as sharing it with a partner?" Mia guessed. Linc nodded solemnly.

The timer she'd set on her phone went off. "Time to remove the ice pack."

Linc grabbed the pack and winced.

"I'm sorry. Does it hurt a lot?"

"It's not too bad. Just throbbing a little at the moment."

He looked so freaking cute sitting there on the exam table trying to not show the pain he was experiencing.

"Don't think about the pain."

"What do you suggest I focus my attention on?"

She didn't think about it. Mia simply acted. She framed his face in her hands. "This," she said and pressed her lips to his.

He let out a surprised gasp, but quickly recovered. One hand came up to the back of her head. He anchored her against him. His lips were so soft, but moved over hers expertly, inciting a delicious shiver.

Somewhere in the back of her mind—the far back—Mia knew that kissing Linc was a horrible decision. But it was easy to push that thought away when his lips were on hers.

The kiss was sending enticing shock waves of pleasure all throughout her.

"One more thing."

They broke apart as the doctor returned. Mia's cheeks heated up. She pressed a hand to them. Linc's face was red. Their gazes met and locked for a long, pregnant moment. But as the doctor walked toward the bed, they broke eye contact. Mia bit her lip, a million thoughts rushing into her mind.

"See," the doctor said, with an ornery look on his face. "I told you that your girlfriend would take care of you."

Mia gulped. Yeah, she'd taken real good care of Linc. She'd only gotten him a sprained ankle. To add to that disaster, she'd gone and kissed him.

She touched a finger to her lips, remembering how good that kiss felt.

The only question left was who was going to take care of her?

Chapter Six

"You're moving in with him?"

Mia paused in the middle of her packing to face her sister and the sound of Emerson's exasperated voice. She knew there would be some concern over her recent decision, but she hadn't anticipated the apprehension on her sister's face.

"I'm not moving in-moving in with him. It's not like we're... you know, or anything."

Cosmo, Emerson and Jack's adorable poodle-mix, jumped onto Mia's bed and let out a small *yip*. In Mia's opinion Cosmo was the cutest dog in all the land with his soft off-white fur and big, human-like green eyes. Mia gave him a full-body rub which set Cosmo's tail into hyperdrive.

Mia and Linc were definitely not moving in the way a couple would. Because Mia and Linc weren't a couple. Not at all. Although, they had kissed. Which she'd forgotten to share with her sister. Forgotten on purpose. Because that kiss had been an amazing, thrilling, toe-curling experience. In fact, if Linc had asked her to move in with him couple-style after that kiss, she wouldn't have hesitated. Hell, she would have done pretty much anything he'd asked after that. Run up and down King Street naked. Jump into the Potomac River in the middle of Winter.

"Hello," Emerson said, waving a hand in front of her face.

"Huh?"

"You are moving in with a man and his two kids."

Mia rolled her eyes. "You make it sound so different than what it really is. I told you. We went dancing last night and he injured his ankle. He needs to stay off it for a couple days. He can work from home, but he needs help with the twins." She rolled up her pajamas and threw them in her open suitcase.

Emerson took the pajamas out and began folding them neatly, while Cosmo grabbed a slipper out of the suitcase and happily chewed on it. "What I don't understand is why you have to be the one to help him out."

"I don't *have* to be."

"I mean, doesn't he have family or friends or something?"

"Em, I offered to help, and he accepted. I don't see why you're getting all angsty about this. I'm a grown woman."

"You are." Emerson paused, biting her lip. She tilted her head and one of her auburn curls fell into her eyes. "But, you're also my baby sister and a woman who has been through so much in the last couple years."

"Em—"

"I don't want to see you get hurt."

"It's probably not me you should be worried about. It's been a very long time since I've baby-sat. Watch out, Hadley and Hugo."

She'd attempted to keep it light. She wanted to ease her sister's mind. But Emerson's frown only deepened.

"You don't have to help out Linc."

"I feel responsible." If Linc hadn't come dancing with her to begin with, he never would have sprained his ankle.

"I get that. I do. But Linc is perfectly capable of hiring someone to help." Emerson folded a shirt that Mia had placed next to her suitcase. "I mean, with all that money he has."

Mia stopped packing again. "What do you mean with all that money?"

"The advantage of being a multi-millionaire."

Mia felt her mouth drop open. She pointed the shoe she'd been packing in Emerson's direction. "Multi-millionaire?"

Emerson looked up. "Duh. Linc. Lincoln McMann. Tech genius."

What in the world was her sister talking about?

"There's no way." Emerson shook her head. "Don't tell me you're clueless about Linc."

"Apparently, I am."

"Linc created this website right out of college with a buddy of his."

"I know about that," Mia said.

"Did you also know that they sold said website a couple years ago for some insane amount of money." Emerson shook her head. "Don't tell me you didn't do any research when you were taking this job."

"I did, but I stuck more to browsing the different pages of the wedding website. I never did background checks on the

95

owners." She threw her shoe into the suitcase and scratched her head. "Linc is rich?"

"Super-rich. Which is why he can afford help if he needs it."

She felt like a total idiot. "I had no idea."

"There's a lot of things you don't know about, Mia."

Mia's first reaction was to be offended by her sister's comment. She wasn't some dumb ingenue. She was a college-educated woman who was nearing the big 3-0. Plus, she'd been married after all.

But Emerson looked serious. More serious than she had seen her in a long time, and any anger she may have harbored dissipated quickly.

"Please don't worry about me, Em. I will be fine. I swear."

Emerson exhaled a long breath. Then she sat down on the bed, crossed her legs, and hugged a pillow to her chest. It was like they were back in high school all over again.

Sensing that someone needed snuggles, Cosmo abandoned the slipper and climbed into Mia's lap. She ran her hands over his soft fur, stopping to scratch behind his ears.

"I know you think you're okay. But I do worry about you because, well…" Emerson bit her lip.

Curious, Mia stopped packing. "What? Spit it out."

"You don't have much experience."

"What exactly do you think is going to happen? It's not like Linc is some villainous character with a long mustache that he twists between his fingers." The image made her giggle. "He's not going to pounce on me. He can't even walk right now."

Emerson reached out and tucked a strand of Mia's hair behind her ear. "Linc isn't the one I'm worried about pouncing."

Those words had Mia pausing. "You think I'm going to take advantage of Linc?"

Emerson shrugged. "Are you?"

Mia sighed. "Em, I just got out of my marriage. A marriage, you will recall, that was awful. There are so many things I want to do. That I *need* to do. For myself. The last thing I want is to fall right back into being a couple."

The worry didn't leave Emerson's face the way Mia had hoped it would. "You're saying the words, but I just have a bad feeling—"

"Stop," she said forcefully. "You have to trust me. I'm a grown woman. I know what I'm doing."

Cosmo let out a bark of solidarity.

"Thank you," Mia said to the adorable dog.

Emerson continued to help her pack. She didn't voice any further concerns, which only caused Mia to think of every possible situation that could occur from her living with Linc for a few days.

Somehow, each scenario ended in a repeat of that kiss.

***

"But why can't you play upstairs?"

Linc looked at his son, and called on all the gods of patience. He'd been fighting this battle all morning. While he lounged on the couch, icing his ankle, Hugo had become determined to get Linc upstairs to play with his Paw Patrol figures. If nothing else, his kids were persistent. That would serve them well later in life.

But right now, Linc could add a throbbing headache to his list of things that hurt on his body.

"Daddy told you," Hadley said, her little hands placed firmly on her hips. "He has a bad ankle, Hugo. It's hard for him to go up the stairs."

Linc could have kissed her.

"Are you going to die?" Hugo asked. Hadley froze, turning worried eyes in his direction.

Linc tried to scoot up on the couch. He reached for each of their hands, pulling them closer. "No, of course not. I just fell last night and hurt my ankle. Other than that, I'm totally fine. And my ankle will be all better in about a week. So there's nothing for the two of you to worry about."

"If you die, who will we live with?" Hugo asked, clearly still worried.

Linc desperately wished they could go back to the "come upstairs and play" conversation. Luckily, Hadley saved the day again. She produced the little medical toy kit Linc had gotten them for their birthdays.

"Daddy said he's not going to die, Hugo. So we have to get him better. Come on. Let's be doctors."

Together, his kids donned their medical outfits. For Hadley, that meant wearing a tutu, a tiara, and the stethoscope from her kit. Hugo wore a Captain America mask and was carrying the toy syringe.

"If you are good, you get a lollypop," Hadley said as she listened to his heart.

"If you're bad, we might have to cut off your leg," Hugo added.

Linc stifled a laugh. He hoped his son didn't go into the medical profession.

"I'll do my best," Linc said seriously.

"It's okay if you cry. Hugo cried at the doctor."

"Did not."

"Did too."

Seeing a fight brewing, Linc quickly jumped in. "Ow, ow, ow. I think my finger is hurt."

Both kids turned their attention to him. "Hugo, get the hammer," Hadley instructed.

And hopefully his daughter would not go into the medical field either.

As his kids got to work "fixing" his finger, Linc leaned back against the cushions, removed his glasses and closed his eyes. His ankle was throbbing. He had a million thoughts about all the things he needed to get done around the house. But there was one thing that was weighing on his mind more than anything else.

Mia.

He'd meant what he said to her when they were in the ER. He had been having fun at the salsa lesson. Until he sprained his ankle, that is. He didn't blame her in any way, shape, or form for his current situation. Instead, he cursed the clumsiness that had been part of his life for as long as he could remember.

But he'd seen how guilty she'd felt. Her face was way too expressive to hold anything back.

When she'd suggested she move in for a few days to help out, he'd answered her quickly. Too quickly. Because he knew she needed to do something to feel like she was helping. So he'd said yes.

Linc groaned. That wasn't why he'd said yes and he knew it. It had nothing to do with Mia's guilt. But he'd rather have Hadley actually cut off his leg than think about the real reason.

It was that kiss. Mia had kissed him. Right there in the ER. She'd said it was to take his mind off his pain. But was that the real reason?

He'd imagined kissing Amelia Dewitt more times than he'd ever be able to count. Never once had he envisioned it happening in the hospital after he made a total fool of himself on a dancefloor.

Yet, he knew better than most that life threw curveballs constantly. The question now was had Mia truly only kissed him to get his mind off his ankle. Or was there more there? Did he want more?

A couple weeks ago, he would have sworn on everything holy that he did not want to be in a relationship. Ever again.

But something about Mia was changing him. And it wasn't just her looks. That would be easy to write off. It was so much more than that.

"We are the best doctors," Hadley announced proudly.

Linc opened his eyes and grinned. "You are pretty darn great."

"Does your finger feel better?" Hugo asked.

Linc glanced down to see his kids had wrapped an ace bandage—where had they gotten that?—around his pointer finger. He held up his hand with his enormously-wrapped finger. It was the size of a grapefruit. "My finger definitely feels better."

Hadley started dancing around the living room. "We are the doctors. We are the doctors," she sang.

"I love playing doctor," Hugo announced.

"Looks like everything is under control here."

Linc almost fell off the couch at the sound of Mia's voice. He righted himself and looked over at her. She was standing at the entrance to the living room, wearing black yoga pants, her pea coat, an orange scarf, and holding an overnight bag, as well as a bag of groceries.

Speaking of playing doctor….

When Mia texted to say she was on her way, he'd told her the code to the front door, so she could let herself in.

He couldn't even get a hello out before his kids went crazy with excitement at this new development.

"Ms. Mia," Hadley squealed. "What are you doing here?"

"Hi, Ms. Mia," Hugo said shyly. His cheeks reddened.

Linc smiled. Seemed like his son had a crush on Mia. Join the club.

Hadley ran to Mia and touched her large overnight bag. "Did you come here to have a sleepover?"

"Are you moving in with us?" Hugo asked. He inched closer to Linc.

"A little bit of both," Mia said with a bell-like laugh.

"Yay!" The kids said in unison before they started firing off questions.

"Do you want to make a tent?"

"Have you ever watched Frozen? What about Beauty and the Beast or Tangled?"

"Do you like ice cream?"

"Can we have ice cream?"

"Are you our new mom?"

Linc choked at the last question. Once again, he scooted up. "Hadley, it's your turn to get the ice pack for me."

Hadley dashed into the kitchen. By the time she returned, Mia had hung her coat on the rack by the door and taken a seat on the loveseat opposite Linc.

"Ms. Mia has graciously offered to stay with us for a couple of days. She's going to help me drive you two monsters to school."

"Want to come to show and tell?" Hadley asked.

Mia smiled. "Well, that sounds amazing. But I do have to go to work too. Maybe we can figure something out."

"Can we have ice cream?" Hugo asked again.

"Can we stay up past our bedtime?"

Here we go. It must be a twin thing, Linc thought, and not for the first time. One of them would start and the other would pick up the conversation. Once they got on a roll, there was no stopping them.

"Can we watch a movie?"

"Can Josh come over?"

"Yeah!" Hadley said, jumping up and down. "And Rachel and Maria?"

"Let's have chocolate for dinner," Hugo said.

"With cake for dessert." Hadley giggled, putting her hands over her mouth.

Linc knew it was time to step in. But before he could, Mia spoke up.

"Chocolate for dinner? That's crazy talk." She made a funny face and both kids laughed. "I was actually going to try and make something special for dinner."

"What?" Hugo asked, intrigued.

"Baked ziti. It's one of my mom's specialties. Growing up, my sister and I loved it. We would beg my mom to make it all the time."

"What is baked ziti?" Hadley asked, suspiciously.

"It's soooo good," Mia said dramatically, batting her lashes. Linc stifled a chuckle. "It's pasta and my mom's special spaghetti sauce. And there's lots of ooey-gooey cheese. Plus, I can make some garlic bread with delicious garlicky butter. Yum, yum, yum."

Linc liked the way she was making basic ingredients sounds amazing and special. He wasn't surprised to see that the kids were captivated by her. He bet their dreams of chocolate and cake were quickly dissipating.

"You can make that?" Hadley asked.

"I can try. I mean, if you want," Mia said nonchalantly.

"I want it," Hugo said.

"Me too."

That settled that. Linc was pleased to see Mia was able to bring the kids back to Earth. No easy feat; he knew that from experience. He knew he needed to step in as well though. Set some ground rules.

"Now that Mia is here and the dinner menu is settled, we need to have a little chat."

"Uh-oh," Hadley said.

Did she just roll her eyes? Wasn't four too young for that? Not for the first time, Linc silently feared what his daughter was going to be like as a teenager.

"Mia is staying with us to help out around here. You two monsters are still going to school. Mia has to go to work."

"What about Devin's house?" Hugo asked.

"Mia will be able to take you to Devin's house for your play date."

"You will?" he asked.

Mia beamed. "Of course. I'll even pick you up and bring you back here too."

Hugo giggled. "Can we get ice cream on the way home?"

Nice try. "We will stick to our normal routine while Mia is here. Everybody understand?" He was using his "stern" voice, something his own father used to do, and he never, ever, ever, in a million years, thought he would do the same.

Both kids nodded.

"Okay, good. That's settled. Now, who wants to show Ms. Mia the guestroom?" Linc asked.

Both kids shot up. "I do. I do." They dashed off, leaving Mia in their wake. She laughed.

As she passed Linc on the couch, he reached out and grabbed her hand. She paused, looking down. Her eyes were shining and her skin was flawless. She looked like a China doll. It stopped his heart.

"You okay?" she asked, glancing quickly at his ankle with the ice pack resting on it. "Do you need something before I find my room?"

He shook his head. "Thank you for doing this."

"You're welcome," she said easily. "It's no problem at all."

He waited a beat. "It's going to be a lot, Mia." He dropped her hand.

Mia bit her lip, obviously considering her words. "Linc, I can handle this."

"Two four-year-olds are a lot to handle." Did she not get that?

"I realize that, Linc. I do. But it's not like you're incapacitated. You sprained your ankle. You will still be present to help me while I'm helping you." She ended with a little laugh.

Her words comforted him, but that giggle did nothing to calm his nerves. He needed to know she was taking this seriously. He was putting his children's safety into her hands.

As if reading his mind, she said, "I would never do anything to put Hugo or Hadley in danger. I promise I will stick to your schedule and make sure they are where they need to be."

"I appreciate that. It's just that…" He couldn't finish the thought. Maybe because he wasn't entirely sure what he wanted to say.

"Honestly, Linc, what could go wrong?"

***

Famous last words, Mia thought of what she'd said to Linc when she'd first arrived. What could go wrong? Um, how about everything.

Mia stood in the middle of a kitchen that resembled a post-disaster location. She'd been trying to make baked ziti because that had been one of her and her sister's favorite meals as kids. And adults, if she was being honest. She'd even called her mom, who had walked her through the recipe. It hadn't seemed hard. Although, her mom had suggested she not try and make the sauce from scratch and just buy a bottle of store-made instead. But the sauce had seemed easy to make too. Some tomatoes, a dash of sugar, sautéed onions and garlic. Easy peasy.

Now, that easy-to-make sauce was absolutely everywhere. Somehow it had bubbled up and out of the pan and was all over the stove. It had splattered up on the microwave. Some of it made it to Linc's beautiful quartz countertops.

She lifted up one of the ziti noodles. The noodle immediately deflated. How in the world had she messed up pasta? Seriously. Besides, cereal and toast, it was the easiest thing to make. Something she'd made for herself countless times. Boil water, insert pasta. Of course, timing it would have helped. But she'd been so concerned with the sauce jumping out of the pan that she'd forgotten to hit the start button on the timer. Then she'd gotten busy trying to find the right baking dish, and…

Ugh. This was a disaster.

She heard Linc before she saw him. The sound of his crutches coming closer had her shoulders deflating and the feeling of a twenty-pound weight sinking in her stomach.

"Whoa," he said when he finally entered the kitchen.

She took a moment. Mia turned off the burners and put a lid over what was left of the sauce. Finally, she turned to face Linc.

She gulped before meeting his eyes. "I'm sorry." She lifted her hands up to take in the kitchen, the mess of the kitchen. But she quickly dropped them. "I'm just so sorry," she repeated.

Linc's gaze swept the room, from the mess at the stove to all the dishes in the sink. Finally, he said, "Ziti not working out?"

"Not so much."

"Mia, have you ever made this recipe before?"

"No, but my mom makes it all the time. And I thought I could...I didn't realize...I failed," she finished, damning her lip for quivering on those last words.

"You didn't fail. You tried."

"I tried and then I failed."

"Trying takes guts."

He was being far too nice to her. "Look at this mess."

"The thing about messes is that they can be cleaned." He hobbled closer. "Can any of this food be salvaged?"

"I don't think so."

"No problem. We'll clean up and then do something else for dinner."

"I don't know what else to make. You know I've been attempting to cook, but my repertoire is pretty limited."

"Again, no problem." He made his way to the freezer, rummaged around for a little while before straightening with a bag dangling from his hand. She took it from him.

"Frozen chicken tenders? But shouldn't the kids get a healthy, homecooked meal?"

Linc smiled, kindness filling his eyes. "Probably. One thing I've learned over the years is that sometimes you have to take the time to be kind to yourself. As much as I wished I could fly and have X-ray vision, I'm not Superman. And sadly, I'm not Superdad."

"But…but…" she stuttered, holding the bag of frozen chicken tenders. "These are frozen."

"They are also shaped like dinosaurs. Trust me, the kids will love them." Linc pointed to the pantry. "In there, I have a jar of sugar-free applesauce, as well as a box of Mac & Cheese."

"Mac & Cheese?" Mia felt exasperated. "Are those shaped like dinosaurs too?"

"Nah. They're Star Wars shapes."

"The kids like Star Wars?"

"I like Star Wars, and maybe it's for me."

She arched an amused eyebrow.

"I'm injured and I want Star Wars Mac & Cheese, okay?"

Mia knew he was kidding, but she couldn't stop her mouth from turning down in a frown. "You are injured. I'm supposed to be here to help you. Instead, you are standing there with your gimpy foot dangling, schooling me on making a damn easy dinner." She blew out a frustrated breath.

Chicken tenders, Mac & Cheese, and applesauce. She shook her head. Here she'd come, so sure of herself. She was going to enter Linc's house and make everything run smoothly for him and the kids. Instead, she was making a mess.

It wasn't that far off from how she'd felt about her marriage. Dinosaur-shaped chicken tenders to a loveless marriage. *I'm losing it.*

But Mia knew she wasn't. It didn't take a shrink to figure out what her angst was about. She'd won countless pageants in her day. She'd been the best cheerleader. Mia won homecoming queen and prom queen in landslides. Even in her sorority, she'd been well-respected and admired.

108

The first thing she'd really failed at was her marriage. She and Charlie hadn't even made it to one year.

Now, she couldn't even cook dinner. The old Amelia would have surely excelled at kitchen skills.

Without realizing it, Linc had limped over to her.

"It's just a dinner," he said softly.

"No, it's not. I mean, look at this place." She gestured around the kitchen. Sauce was all over the stovetop. She'd used almost every pot and pan Linc owned. "I made such a mess, and it's not even like there's a good dinner to show for my efforts."

"What's really going on in here?" Linc tapped her head.

She didn't know why, but something about his caring and soft voice undid her. She felt the tears bubbling up and did everything in her power to keep them inside.

But when Linc reached for her, folding her into his strong arms for a long, comforting hug, she let the stupid tears come. Only a few, but no less embarrassing.

"I'm sorry. I'm sorry. I'm the one who's supposed to be comforting you," she mumbled against his shirt.

She felt Linc chuckle. "Mia, I merely sprained my ankle. While I would welcome any comforting you'd like to do, it's not really necessary. Now, driving the kids around? That I can use."

"I suck." It was all she could think to say.

Linc's arms tightened around her. "Let's sit down for a minute," he said, releasing her and nodding toward the kitchen table.

She followed him to it, helping him situate his crutches.

"Will the kids be upset they aren't getting the dinner I described earlier?"

"Nah. Kids move on quickly. Besides, I happen to know that dinosaur-shaped chicken tenders is one of Hugo's favorite meals. Plus, I say we give them that ice cream they've been wanting for dessert. I have a pint of chocolate in the freezer."

She was frowning again. She couldn't help it.

"Mia, it's just a dinner," he repeated.

"It's more than that." She sniffled.

"Tell me." His light brown eyes were searching her face, probably attempting to figure out what had made her go looney tunes over one recipe gone bad. She realized he had very kind eyes. Something about them penetrated her emotions, and she found herself opening up.

"I won Little Miss Virginia Sweetie-Pie when I was five years old."

He didn't even flinch at her strange comment. "Impressive." He waited patiently.

"I won a lot of other things too."

"Yes, you did. I remember from high school."

She nodded. "In fact, I excelled at pretty much everything I ever tried. Nothing was hard for me."

"Mia, do you honestly think anyone remembers that you were Little Miss Virginia Sweetie-Pie? Do you think it's important that you stood out in the middle of our high school football stadium as you were crowned homecoming queen?"

"Well, I…I don't know."

"Those things are great. Don't get me wrong. I'm not trying to take anything away from you, or young Amelia. But, those wins aren't you. They are just things you did and accomplished. They're not who you are."

"They're who I was."

"Amelia Dewitt. You're Mia now." He covered her hand with his. "Maybe Amelia never stepped a toe out of line. Maybe Amelia did everything to a gold standard. But Mia is allowed to make mistakes."

She let out a breath she'd been holding most of her life. She was allowed to make mistakes? She didn't have to be perfect?

What a strange concept.

What a freeing thought.

"Except for my sister, you're the only person who's ever said anything like that to me before."

"I didn't mean to—"

"Thank you," she interrupted him. "You don't know what it means to me." She turned her hand over, connecting their fingers. "You're amazing."

He squeezed her fingers and leaned closer. "So are you. You always have been."

"I'm amazing even when I'm making a huge mess?" She jerked her head in the direction of the stove area.

His gaze flicked down to her mouth. "Especially then."

Mia felt herself being pulled in. Ever since she'd arrived, she'd tried her best to not think about their kiss from the night before. She knew that kissing Linc again would muddy the waters even more, and that could spell disaster for their current situation.

But she couldn't stop her own eyes from taking in his lips. She cursed herself and looked up to meet his eyes. Eyes that had darkened. Eyes that were full of lust.

She swallowed hard. Even as she told herself to stop, she was inching forward.

Linc reached out and cupped her cheek. She leaned her head into his hand, his touch comforting, yet, thrilling at the same time.

This was wrong, so wrong. But she wanted to kiss him more than she wanted to breathe.

They were so close that she could feel his warm breath on her face. Her lips parted and both of their eyes began to close.

"Daddy, Hadley shoved me."

They both jumped back in their chairs as the twins rushed into the kitchen at full speed.

"Did not," Hadley said. "I was just showing him where to stand."

Linc kept his eyes on hers for a moment more. Something flashed over his face. Was it...disappointment?

Finally, he turned to his fighting children. "Hadley, did you show Hugo where to stand by shoving him?"

"No." Hadley looked indignant at first, and then completely guilty.

Mia stifled a laugh.

"I should get to push her back," Hugo said.

"That's not how life works," Linc said patiently.

"Why?"

Linc exhaled loudly. "Sometimes you have to let things go."

As Linc spoke to the kids, Mia rose. She wanted to start cleaning the kitchen before she made their new and improved dinner.

She knew she should follow Linc's parental advice and let things go too. Mainly, she needed to release this need to kiss him. To touch him. To be around him.

Their situation was already complicated. They were coworkers. She was helping him while he was injured. He was a single dad. She was trying to find her path in life. The last thing either of them needed was romance.

She found some cleaner under the sink. When she straightened, she turned and looked at Linc.

She wanted him. Despite it all.

Hadley had started singing "Let It Go" from *Frozen*. The lyrics ran through Mia's head. In fact, they went in one ear and right back out the other.

No matter what, Mia just didn't think she could let go of her feelings for Linc.

Chapter Seven

"Where's Hadley?" Mia asked as she walked into the living room. Linc was on the couch, icing his ankle. She could hear Hugo playing in the other room.

Mia felt much better than she had after her failed attempt at baked ziti the night before. Linc had been right. She'd thrown together his food suggestions and the kids went nuts. They couldn't be more excited for chicken tenders and mac & cheese. Not to mention the chocolate ice cream for dessert. You would have thought she'd offered them all the free toys in the world.

She wished she could still get that excited over the little things. Maybe she should take a page out of their books.

The kids had woken early, and Mia spent some time watching cartoons with them before making a successful breakfast. Hard to screw up cereal and toast though. Still, she would take the victory.

After cleaning up the kitchen, making sure Linc was set on the couch with coffee and an ice pack, she'd run up to the guest room, showered and dressed for the day.

Linc shifted on the sofa. "Hadley is next door. There's a little girl her age who lives there. They play all the time."

"That's nice. We had a lot of kids in our neighborhood when I was growing up," Mia said.

The front door opened and slammed shut just then. Hadley entered the living room, the scowl evident on her face.

Linc pushed away from the couch cushions. "How did you get back over here?"

"Mrs. Sheila walked me back."

Linc relaxed. Hadley crossed her arms over her chest.

"How was Ramona's house?" Linc asked, taking a sip of coffee from one his oversized coffee mugs.

Hadley kicked at something unseen on the ground. "'kay."

Uh-oh, Mia thought. She wondered if the girls had gotten in a fight.

"You weren't over there for very long," Linc said, clearly unaware that his daughter was upset.

Hadley sighed loudly. "Ramona and her mom are going shopping. I don't care anyway."

Ah, now Mia understood. She watched Linc, trying to see if he would catch on to the real problem. His blank face was a big no.

"I wouldn't want to go shopping with my mom, even if I did have one."

Linc's face drained of color. Finally, he got it. Mia felt for him. What a tough situation. Linc had to play the roles of both father and mother, and currently he couldn't even do those to the best of his ability due to his bum ankle.

It didn't take more than a second for Mia to make up her mind. While Linc tried to soothe his upset daughter, Mia jumped up.

"Hey, Hadley. I was thinking of getting my nails done today. You wouldn't want to come with me, would you?"

Hadley turned green eyes in Mia's direction so wide they resembled Linc's coffee cups. "You're getting your nails done? Like with paint and stuff?" Hadley asked reverently.

Mia stifled a giggle. "Yep. Would you like to get yours done too? I mean, if you wouldn't mind coming with me. I just really hate going to the salon by myself."

Mia prayed her usual nail salon could fit in two last minute appointments on a Saturday.

"I could get my nails painted too?" Hadley asked quietly.

"Sure. If that's okay with your dad," Mia quickly added when she remembered she needed to check with Linc.

"Oh pleaseeeee, Daddy, pleaseeee. Can I get my nails done too?"

Mia snuck a glance at Linc who was looking at his daughter with nothing less than eternal love. It was such a sweet moment. Mia wished she had a camera to capture it.

Then Linc shifted and met her gaze. His expression changed completely.

"Yes, you can go get your nails painted," Linc said, never taking his eyes off Mia.

"After we get our nails painted, we could go see a movie or get dinner," Mia continued since she was on a roll.

Her mind was flying with ideas; cute things to take Hadley to do. There was an adorable tea house that served high tea with scones and cakes and the whole works. Unfortunately, they would definitely not be able to get a reservation at this point. But there was a new kids movie out in theaters.

It dawned on Mia that the living room was completely quiet. She glanced over at Hadley, who was bouncing up and down excitedly and too thrilled to actually make a sound. Next thing she knew, Hadley flew across the room and launched herself at Mia. Mia happily picked her up for a long hug. "I guess that's a yes."

Over Hadley's head, she met Linc's gaze again and froze. He was staring in their direction, his eyes bouncing between her and his daughter. As Hadley squealed and immediately began talking a million miles an hour, Linc put a hand to his heart. His eyes softened. He met Mia's gaze and nodded. She could see him swallowing hard.

Thank you, he mouthed.

Mia had won pageants and contests galore. But this was, by far, the best recognition she'd ever received.

***

Mia had never seen anyone as excited as Hadley was to have a girls' day. It was absolutely adorable. She'd spent a long time agonizing over the perfect outfit. Finally, with Mia's help, she'd settled on a light blue dress and her favorite "sparkle shoes."

Linc told her she looked like a princess and Hadley had giggled and twisted back and forth so her dress swirled around her.

For a moment, Mia had worried that Hugo would feel left out. But he'd taken one look at his sister and said he didn't like getting dressed up. Then he ran to the playroom and seemed quite content to play with his Legos.

"Call if you need anything. Or if Hadley doesn't behave. Or if you—"

"Linc," Mia said laughing. "We'll be fine."

"If you're sure," he said, not sounding sure at all.

To be honest, Mia was a bit nervous. She used to babysit kids all the time in her earlier days, but it had been quite some time since she spent an entire day with a little one all by herself. But she didn't want Linc to worry any more than he was already, so she put on a brave face.

"Of course I'm sure. Hadley and I are going to have so much fun. Right, Had?"

"Yes. Come on. Let's go." Hadley latched on to Mia's hand and tugged hard.

Mia laughed, waving at Linc over her shoulder as Hadley dragged her out the door and toward the car. Linc had offered for her to use his SUV. Hadley and Hugo were both still in car seats and it would be easier than transferring the seat to her car.

After she started the car, she swiveled in her seat to take in a beaming Hadley. "You ready, Freddy?"

Hadley giggled and punched her fists in the air. "Yay!"

And off they went. Luckily, she'd been going to the same nail salon for years, so everyone knew her name. They were more than happy to help accommodate appointments for both her and Hadley.

Everyone in the salon made a big fuss over Hadley, and she ate up the attention.

"This is my first mani and pedi," she announced proudly, as Mia removed Hadley's coat and hung it on a rack by the door.

"Then we need to make sure your nails look extra special," one of the nail technicians said. "Why don't you go over to that wall and pick the colors you would like to use? And if you want sparkles on top, we can do that too."

"Sparkles," Hadley said reverently.

"Come on, sweetie," Mia said, taking her hand and leading her to the large wall full of every color ever imagined. "You can pick your colors and then you can help me pick my colors."

"Really?" Hadley squealed. "I can pick what you will get too?"

"Sure."

Ten minutes later, Mia was slightly regretting allowing a four-year-old to pick her nail polish. Mia would be getting a neon green on her toes, and Hadley instructed that sparkles be put on top. Well, at least that was just on her toes. No doubt she'd keep her toes firmly covered until the ground thawed in the Spring. As for her fingernails, she would be getting a deep purple, again with sparkles. The color wasn't actually bad. But it definitely wasn't something Mia would have picked for herself.

After much deliberation, Hadley decided to get a "really pretty pink" color. Of course, sparkles would be added to both her toes and fingers.

Hand-in-hand, they made their way to the pedicure chairs. Mia helped Hadley get into hers. The nail technician gave her a couple pillows to put behind Hadley's back, so she would be able to reach the basin of water at her feet.

Once they got Hadley settled, Mia removed her shoes and socks and sat back in the chair with a magazine. A magazine that she didn't even have a chance to crack open before Hadley turned to her.

"Are you going to marry Daddy?"

Mia choked on the water she'd just sipped. "What?"

"Daddy isn't married. You aren't married either. How come you're not married?"

"Um…"

"Have you ever been married?" Hadley tilted her head.

"Well…"

"Daddy was married to mommy. But then she left."

Hm. Mia couldn't deny that she was curious what had happened between Linc and his ex-wife. He never mentioned her, and until right now, the twins didn't either. How unusual to not have a mother in the picture with two four-year-olds.

"Have you been married?" Hadley repeated. Finally, she paused to give Mia a chance to answer.

"Yes, I was married. But not for very long."

"You got divorced," Hadley said, nodding her head wisely.

"Correct. I didn't want to get divorced, but sometimes that happens."

"How long did you have to talk to the lawyers and the judge?"

Until now, Viv, one of the nail technicians, had remained discreetly quiet. But even she looked up at Mia in response

120

to Hadley's question. They exchanged a look. Mia blew out a long breath.

"What do you mean, sweetie?" Mia wasn't sure what Hadley was talking about exactly.

"Daddy had to talk to the lawyer man every day," Hadley said conversationally. "Then Daddy and the lawyer man had to go to the judge to talk about cus-a-dee."

Oh no. Now Mia understood. Linc had fought for custody. Knowing how protective Linc was of the kids, she doubted he would have shared any of that with his daughter.

"How do you know about all of that?" she asked Hadley.

Hadley shrugged. "I hear things," she said simply.

Man, anyone who thought kids weren't paying attention was clearly delusional.

"And my friend, Sue's, parents got divorced too. They have lawyers."

Mia frowned. How sad that kids this young were hearing about divorce and judges and lawyers. They should be playing with their toys and having fun. Of course, she wasn't completely naïve. Mia had to assume this was the new normal.

"Sue's daddy cheated on her mommy."

Again, Viv exchanged a look with Mia. "Wow. That's a lot of information you have."

"I listen," Hadley said.

Mia leaned over and tugged lightly on one of Hadley's curls. "Just like a grown up." Hadley giggled.

Without warning, the little girl completely changed the direction of her conversation and began to tell Mia all about a cartoon she watched at her friend Ramona's house last week.

Mia couldn't stop her thoughts from straying though. Should she tell Linc about Hadley's comments? She worried her lip as she considered.

If she did bring it up, would Linc elaborate on the divorce and the situation with his wife? Did the kids still see her? Surely, they must.

After their nails and toes were done and looking fabulous, Mia checked the time on her phone. There was still quite a bit of time before the movie started.

"What are we going to do?" Hadley asked, as they left the salon. Hadley was waving to all of the people, as if she were a real-life princess. Mia stifled a giggle.

"I have an idea. Did I ever tell you what my mom does?"

Hadley shook her head.

"She owns a bridal shop. That's where brides go to pick out their wedding dress. Would you like to see it?"

Hadley's eyes widened, and she started jumping up and down. "Brides!" she squealed. "Will we see any brides? Will they have the dresses on? Can I try one on?"

Mia took Hadley's hand and steered her in the direction of Dewitt's Bridal.

If Mia thought the women at the nail salon made a big deal over Hadley, that was nothing compared to the welcome at her mother's shop. Beatrice Dewitt loved children and she practically scooped Hadley up as soon as she entered the store.

"Sorry, Mama, I know Saturdays are your busiest, but I thought Hadley might like to see the dresses."

"Hush. It's just fine that you're both here. Would you like some cookies?" she asked Hadley.

"Oh, yes, please," Hadley said politely.

"How about champagne? We always give our brides and their families champagne."

"What is champagne?" Hadley asked.

"Uh, Mama?"

Beatrice ignored her. She took Hadley by the hand and led her to one of the many seating areas in the store. While she ran off to get the yummy butter cookies she always kept on hand, the other sales people all stopped by to make a fuss over Hadley.

Beatrice returned with a silver tray. On it were the cookies, some grapes, a small vase of flowers, and a champagne flute.

"Mama," Mia whispered.

"Stop worrying. It's Ginger Ale. Hadley is here for the bridal experience."

"You do realize she's four and not an actual bride."

"Hush," Beatrice said again.

Everyone was asking Hadley questions, and the little girl was smiling and giggling. They were showing her dresses and letting her try on tiaras and veils. Beatrice even pulled out some of the flower girl dresses she kept in stock and Hadley did a fashion show. Everyone in the store, even the brides, oohed and ahhed as she came out of the dressing room.

Mia showed Hadley how to walk on a runway. She held her hand as they turned and posed. Her mother snapped pictures on her phone.

Hadley insisted Mia try on a veil too. When she looked in the large mirror, Mia felt a flutter in her stomach. She wore a cathedral-length veil with lace around the edges. Hadley had on one of Mia's favorite flower girl gowns. It was an ivory dress with flower accents, meant to compliment one of the bridal gowns that she absolutely adored.

As she looked at the two of them in the mirror, Hadley reached for her hand. It could have been her wedding. Hadley could be her flower girl.

Which meant she could be marrying Linc.

Mia gulped and put a hand to her stomach. Marrying Linc. Becoming a mother to Hadley and Hugo. She waited for the nerves or some kind of anxiety to wash over her. Strangely, nothing did. She felt fine. In fact, her lips turned up and she grinned ear-to-ear.

"Well, look at the two of you. Quite stunning," her mother said.

"Ms. Mia is the bride," Hadley said. "And I'm the flower girl. And princess."

Beatrice laughed. "Yes, you are. Would the princess like another cookie?"

Hadley jumped up and down. "Yes, yes, yes." She ran off toward the tray of cookies and left Mia standing alone with the gorgeous veil and a million questions.

"You will make the most beautiful bride," Beatrice said.

Mia frowned. "I've already been a bride."

Beatrice stepped forward and gently put a hand to Mia's cheek. "And you will be one again."

"Mama—"

"You're so young, Amelia. Marrying Charlie was a mistake. But I know you are going to find your Prince Charming. Maybe you're on your way now."

Mia stayed silent. She didn't want to acknowledge her mother's statement. Luckily, she didn't have time to respond because Hadley bounded over.

"Is it time for the movie yet, Ms. Mia?"

Saved by the bell-like voice of a four-year-old.

After she helped Hadley change back into her clothes, they spent twenty minutes saying goodbye to everyone in the store. Hadley hugged Beatrice for a long time. Mia liked seeing her mother with a little kid. She would be an amazing grandmother. Mia wondered if her sister and Jack had talked about having kids yet.

They finally left the shop and headed to the movie theater. Mia bought Hadley popcorn and candy and they settled in to watch the kids' flick. Hadley absolutely loved it.

After the movie, they went to one of Mia's favorite Italian restaurants. She taught Hadley how to dunk her bread in olive oil. When the waitress came over to take their drink orders, Mia had to stifle a laugh.

"Yes, I would like a glass of champagne please."

The waitress's mouth fell open and she glanced at Mia.

"You don't want to have too much champagne in one day," she said to Hadley. "But how about a Shirley Temple?"

The waitress relaxed. "With extra cherries," she said with a wink at Hadley.

Halfway through dinner, Mia realized something. She was having fun. She was really enjoying herself. She wasn't doing any of the things on her list, and yet, she hadn't laughed and smiled this much since before she'd been married.

It was nice to have Hadley with her. She'd been a little nervous to spend the whole day with a four-year-old, but the two of them had gotten along like they were… Mia didn't want to finish that thought. It was silly, and it wasn't where she was headed in life. Was it?

Mother and daughter.

Hm. Children. She wasn't sure how to feel about that concept. A lot of her friends from Clemson and Kappa either had children already or were just beginning to start their families. Of course, none of them had just ended a six-month-long marriage.

"This is the best day of my life," Hadley said.

Mia glanced at Hadley's big smile. She'd gone to parties, learned how to salsa dance, and completed some of the other things from her to-do list. Yet, it wasn't until this very moment that she actually felt like she'd accomplished something worthwhile.

Chapter Eight

Linc could tell his son was restless. But since he knew Hugo as well as the back of his hand, he knew to sit back and wait. Hugo would come to him when he was good and ready.

For now, he was lounging on the couch, his foot elevated on a pillow. The timer on his phone went off and Linc removed the ice pack from his ankle.

He idly flipped through the channels on the television. Nothing was catching his eye, until he saw that Star Wars, Episode IV was set to start in a half hour. A quick look through the guide told him it would be followed with episodes V and VI. Game on. Linc had a plan for his Saturday.

That's when Hugo walked into the room.

"Hey, buddy, what's going on?" he asked.

Hugo flung himself over an ottoman dramatically. "Nothing."

"Yeah, same here," Linc said, trying to commiserate.

"What do you think Hadley's doing?"

Linc smiled. His kids were definitely different from each other and he'd refereed countless fights between them. But when it came down to it, they loved each other, and neither of them liked being apart from the other for too long. He wasn't sure how long that would last, but for right now, it warmed his heart.

"I don't know. Probably girly stuff." Linc made a face like he was gagging and Hugo laughed. His son came over and crawled on top of him.

"Stupid girly stuff," Hugo said.

"Yeah. I'm glad we're here. Two men hanging out."

"Two strong men." Hugo put his arm up and showed his muscles. Linc made a big production out of being impressed with his son's strength.

They laughed some more over the fact that they were burly men and didn't ever want to do girl stuff, when Hugo veered off in a completely different direction that Linc never saw coming.

"Is Mommy ever coming back?"

"Uh…"

"Is she?" Hugo asked, more urgently this time.

Linc took a long moment to collect himself. He'd read what felt like hundreds of parenting books. He visited parenting blogs and Facebook groups. But none of those things ever prepared him for questions like this. It wasn't often one of the kids would bring up their mother, but when they did, it hit him right in the chest every single time.

"Do you want Mommy to come back?"

Hugo shrugged. "I dunno. I don't really remember her."

"Would you like to see some pictures or videos?"

Perusing old pictures of Chrissy was not his idea of a good time, but he always made sure to have some around so the kids could see their mother.

"Nah." Hugo was picking at some lint on the afghan that was covering Linc. "Do you think Mommy would be mad that Ms. Mia is here helping take care of us?"

Hell yes. Of course, Linc would never say that out loud. Chrissy had a jealous streak. More than that, she didn't like to be outshone. And in two short days, Mia had outdone her on mother duty by leaps and bounds.

"I don't think so," Linc lied. "Daddy hurt his ankle and he needed some help taking care of monster number one and monster number two." He tickled Hugo who broke out into laughter.

But when the giggles died down, Hugo had more questions. "How come Aunt Nadine couldn't come watch us?"

"Well…"

"Ms. Mia came instead," Hugo said.

"Yes…"

"I like her. Do you like her?"

Linc felt like he was being grilled. "I do like her."

"Are you going to kiss her?"

Linc choked. "What?"

"Hadley said that when two people like each other that they kiss and then they get married."

"Well, that's true sometimes. But not always." Linc knew he was floundering.

"And then they go live in a castle."

"There are all different kinds of houses." He coughed and tried to gain control of the conversation. "Be honest with me. Are you okay with Ms. Mia being here in our house?"

"Yep. She's nice. Are you going to get married?"

He hoped not. As far as he was concerned, marriage led to divorce. Linc couldn't stomach the mere thought of going through another divorce. "Maybe someday. But I don't know for sure. And it might not be to Ms. Mia."

"But it might be with Ms. Mia?" Curiosity coated the question.

"Who knows. But I can promise you one thing. If, and when, I ever get married, and no matter who I'm marrying, you and Hadley are the most important people in the world to me. I will make sure that both of you like who I'm marrying and that you are happy and safe and healthy."

Truer words he could never say. He had to hold back on the passion that he felt bubbling up inside of him just thinking of his kids. He loved them so much.

"Okay," Hugo said simply.

"Any other questions for me?"

"Can we go to Disney World?"

A little off topic, but, in general, a great change in conversation.

"It's a possibility."

"Yay! When?"

Linc let out a laugh. Kids were relentless. But he knew better than to mention Disney World. "We'll talk about it."

"When?" Hugo repeated.

"When your sister is present." Time to divert. "In the meantime, I have a special treat for you."

Hugo cocked his head, interest clearly shining in his eyes. "What is it? Can we go swimming?"

"Let's keep swimming in January down to a minimum. No, this is a much better treat."

Hugo started bouncing up and down. "What? What is it?"

This was something Linc had wanted to do with his kids for a long, long time. He'd done it with his father.

"We're going to watch Star Wars."

Linc checked the time and saw they still had about ten minutes to go before his favorite movie began. So, he hobbled into the kitchen on his crutches and made some microwave popcorn. Hugo helped him gather a few other snacks. They might as well go big.

Back in the family room, Linc put his arm around Hugo. The bowl of popcorn was on the coffee table. They had their juice boxes. It was movie time.

"A long time ago in a galaxy far away…"

Didn't matter how many times he'd seen it, or which movie it was, but watching the words scroll up the screen always got him excited. That's when he realized something. His son was four. His son couldn't read. Shoot.

Linc leaned over and began reading the words to Hugo, who settled back against him, awe over the fantasy movie written all over his face.

Linc knew the feeling. He could still vividly remember the first time he'd watched this.

He may not have a wife and his kids may be motherless, but sometimes everything just seemed to work out. Everything was fine. Just fine.

**

When dinner was over, Mia and Hadley headed back to Linc's house. Hadley burst in the door, immediately sharing all the details of her day. Seeming bored, Hugo went back to the coloring book he'd been scribbling in when they'd entered.

For his part, she could tell Linc was trying to keep up. He was nodding along as Hadley gestured and giggled. He did perk up when Hadley revealed an interesting little tidbit.

"And then Miss Beatrice gave me champagne."

He turned to Mia and arched an eyebrow.

Ginger ale, she mouthed and Linc relaxed.

"Well, it sounds like you had a wonderful day."

"It was the best day ever," Hadley said.

"What do you say to Ms. Mia?"

Mia expected a thank you. Instead, Hadley wrapped her arms around Mia's legs and looked up at her with those big, irresistible eyes. "I love you."

Mia and Linc exchanged a glance. Neither of them knew what to say. Finally, Linc cleared his throat. "Can you tell Ms. Mia thank you?"

"Thank you, Ms. Mia."

Mia picked her up and gave her a real hug. "You're welcome." She whispered in the little girl's ear. "I love you too."

"We got our nails down," Hadley said to her brother, wiggling her fingers in front of his unimpressed face.

"Well, we had a man's day."

Hadley started, her fingers pausing in mid-air. "What does that mean?"

"It was awesome," Hugo said, finally putting his crayons down. "We ate junk food and watched Star Wars."

Mia had to stifle a laugh when Hadley actually rolled her eyes. She didn't realize kids started that gesture so young. Hadley also did her best impression of turning her nose up. "Oh yeah? Well, we ate a grownup dinner at a fancy restaurant."

"Did you have popcorn?"

"We did at the movies," Hadley said. "And I tried on wedding dresses because I'm a princess and I'm going to be a bride."

If Mia wasn't mistaken, Linc's face lost a little bit of color at his daughter's statement. "Bride?" He scratched his head. "Aren't you a little young for that?"

"No." Hadley put her hands on her hips. "Ms. Mia's mom said I made a beautiful bride."

"I took her over to my mom's shop after we got our nails down. That's where she had the champagne too."

"First champagne, then marriage talk." Linc seemed bemused. "Well, who are you going to marry, Had?"

Hadley sat on the ottoman, delicately fluffing her dress around her legs. "I'm not sure yet. Maybe Josh or Tyler. But there is Oliver too."

"Yuck." Hugo made his best disgusted face. "Can we watch Star Wars again?"

Linc beamed with pride. "You are definitely my son. While I would love nothing more than to watch another movie, I'm afraid it's…bedtime," Linc said to Hadley and Hugo's groans. "Everyone upstairs."

"Dad, will you read me the Superman book?" Hugo asked.

"I don't want to read that book," Hadley said. "I want to read the princess book."

"Gross. I don't want to hear about princesses again."

Poor kid, Mia thought. Even though Hadley was outnumbered by two males, she clearly ran the roost. "How about everyone changes into their PJ's and brushes their teeth. Then, Hugo can come down here and read the Superman book with Daddy. I'll read the princess book with Hadley upstairs."

"Yay." And both kids flew up the stairs.

"You have no idea the argument you just stopped. I am forever in your debt."

"How often do they fight over bedtime stories?" she asked.

Linc groaned. "Two kids with two very different sets of interests." He shoved a thumb toward his chest. "One dad."

One parent. It had to be incredibly difficult.

"About today," Linc began, running a hand through his hair. He paused for a long moment. "I can't tell you what it means…that is, what you did was…I'm really grateful."

Mia smiled. She wasn't sure what to say, but it didn't matter. Before she could open her mouth, Hugo was calling for help. She nodded at Linc and rushed up the stairs.

After everyone's teeth were brushed and favorite jammies put on, she read Hadley's book of choice. Halfway through the story, Hadley's eyes began to flutter closed and her breathing slowed. She whispered, "I wish you were my mother." Then she turned onto her side and closed her eyes.

Mia remained where she was for a long time. She didn't know what to think. She was at such an interesting point in her life. She was a divorced woman who was finally finding herself. That's why it was so important to try new things and have exciting adventures. She supposed sharing a girls' day with Hadley counted as new and exciting.

She was exhausted. Hanging out with Hadley was tiring for sure. The little girl had so much energy. It was certainly infectious, if not draining.

Mia closed the book and put it back on the book shelf. Then she returned to Hadley and tucked the blankets around her. She couldn't resist running a hand over Hadley's soft curls. She watched the little girl's slow and even breathing.

Taking a long, deep breath, Mia took a step back. She needed to remember that this wasn't permanent. She was only staying with Linc and the kids for a few days. Then she would be returning to her life. The life that she'd earned. The life that she wanted to live. On her terms. Finally.

Slowly, she backed out of the room, making sure to leave the door open halfway.

Maybe Mia hadn't done something from her adventure list today. But somehow, she felt something she hadn't in a long, long time. Content.

***

Linc had never seen his daughter more excited, and that was saying something since Hadley was a ball of enthusiasm on a normal day. He didn't know how he would ever be able to repay Mia for what she did today.

After he read a story to Hugo, Mia had taken the sleepy boy up to bed. Now, Linc laid back against the pillows of the couch and closed his eyes. He was in unchartered territory. There was a woman in the house. His kids were happy. Happier than he'd ever seen them.

As for him, well, despite a sore ankle, he was…feeling things. Things he hadn't expected to feel ever again. More like, he hadn't wanted to feel ever again.

Mia was more than attractive. She was that unattainable crush from his adolescence. That was such an impressionable period of life. Mia would always rank higher than other women.

Still, when she'd reentered his life, Linc had remained firm. He could find her attractive. He could enjoy hanging out with her; laughing at work, sharing lunches, even helping her with her to-do list. But he would never allow himself to fall for her. Because the idea of falling for any woman was terrifying. The mere idea filled him with dread. It wasn't the relationship that scared him. It was what came after. All the fallout. The hurt feelings, the devastation and loss. It wasn't only him. He had two children to consider now. Maybe—and it was a gigantic maybe—he could go through that kind of pain again. But there was no way on this planet he would ever expose his kids to that.

It was settled. He had to put a wall up between him and Mia.

He smelled her before he saw her. She'd taken a shower after putting the kids to bed. He'd heard the water running. A scent of flowers wafted down the stairs right before he heard her footsteps. It was like he had walked into a summer garden.

She appeared at the bottom of the stairs wearing a pair of comfortable-looking gray pants and a Clemson t-shirt that seemed to be on the older side. Her hair was damp and her face was scrubbed clean of makeup. Somehow she was even more beautiful without makeup. There was a vulnerability to her that was intriguing. She wasn't naïve, but rather, she was just a good person. That goodness shone through her pretty blue eyes and all of that fresh, rosy skin.

That wall that he'd just erected came crumbling down around him. It never stood a chance.

She smiled. "Hey." She walked to him and took a seat at the opposite end of the couch. Before she could finish pulling her feet up into a cross-leg position, he spotted something. He could only stare.

She tilted her head. "What?"

"Wow, check out those toes."

"What? Oh." Mia laughed. She uncrossed her legs, wiggled her toes, and then quickly re-crossed them and covered herself up with a throw blanket.

"That blanket's not going to help. I think they can be seen from space." Linc laughed.

She leaned over and hit him lightly in the shoulder. "Shut up. I'll have you know this color was your daughter's pick."

Linc grew serious. He studied her face, searching for some sign of annoyance or displeasure. But Mia was beaming. "You enjoyed yourself today?" It was more question than statement. He was vaguely aware of holding his breath while he waited for her answer.

"I really did."

"Seriously?"

She nodded emphatically. "Hadley is just so...adorable," she decided. "My mom used to take me and Emerson out for days like that. Sometimes we would go shopping, or get our hair done, or go into D.C. and visit a museum, and then have, as Hadley said, 'a fancy grown-up dinner' in a restaurant our parents didn't usually take us." She looked off into the distance. "We always had the best time. It actually meant a lot to me to do the same kind of thing with Hadley."

Linc felt like his heart might burst. "I can't thank you enough for taking her out for a girls' day. It meant so much to her. We're going to be hearing all the details for a long time."

Once again, she focused her gaze on him. "It was my pleasure, Linc. Really."

He glanced down to where her toes were hidden and a smile formed. "Still, I know she can be a handful."

"She's wonderful. So is Hugo." She bit her lip and glanced down. "Just like their daddy."

Had he thought his heart was going to burst? Linc was pretty sure it already had. He raised a hand, but wasn't sure why, so he let it fall to his lap. "Mia," he said with a pleading note. He didn't know what he was imploring her to do, only that he needed something in that moment.

I need her to stop looking at me with those fathomless eyes. I need her to stop biting her lip because it draws my attention to her mouth. The mouth I want to kiss.

"Mia," he said again.

He saw her chest rise and fall. "I'm sorry, Linc, but you are amazing. What you've done with your kids is absolutely awe-inspiring."

Like any parent, he loved hearing compliments about his kids. But there was something even more exciting when Mia was the one doing the complimenting.

"I appreciate that much more than I can say," he said in a gruff voice. Emotions were rising and he wasn't sure how to take that.

"I wouldn't say it if it weren't true." She moved closer. "When I think about who you were back in high school and where you are now, I'm just so happy for you. You've built a really amazing life for your family."

A family that was incomplete. For now. Maybe forever.

Linc couldn't help himself. He shifted so he could move closer to Mia.

"I don't want to complicate your life, Linc," she whispered.

Once again, his gaze focused on those lips. "Never in my wildest dreams would I have thought you and I would be sitting here like this."

Lightly, she touched a hand to his chest. "I know. Two months ago, I was, well, not in a very good place."

Her words were a potent reminder that she had also been through a rough patch in life. Maybe she didn't have children, but Mia could understand the feelings that came with ending a marriage. The disappointment, the anger, the resentment, the confusion, the hurt, and that potent feeling of failure.

Perhaps it was because of that commonality, or maybe it was just the way her blue eyes had darkened, but Linc couldn't stop it. Had he really tried to put a wall up? What a joke.

He framed her face and gently pressed his lips to hers. She let out a little sigh that was more appealing than he could have ever imagined.

Her hand on his chest tightened, clutching his shirt. He moved his lips over hers gently. This kiss wasn't about passion or speed. It was about a connection; a connection that he was shocked they had between them.

She tasted sweet. That garden scent continued to infiltrate his senses, swirling around him so that he was surrounded by a flowery cocoon.

When they finally broke apart, she offered a shy smile. "That was nice."

It was way more than nice. But Linc kept that to himself.

"Yes," he agreed, but felt stupid saying.

She rose, folding the blanket and placing it on the back of the couch. "I think I should go to bed."

"Mia—"

"I meant what I said. I don't want to be a complication for you, Linc. I don't regret that kiss. In fact, I wanted it to happen."

Oh god, so did he. He had to admit that to himself now.

Her smile grew. "Good night, Linc."

"Good night, Mia."

He watched her ascend the stairs. Linc rubbed a finger over his lips, still feeling Mia's soft lips.

What was happening? Was he actually starting to open his heart again? Speaking of, he swore his heart just let out a little flutter.

Linc fell back against the couch cushions with a loud groan. This was the worst timing ever. He wasn't in a place to fall for someone again. Under no circumstances did he want to go down that road again. The road that led to heartache.

His lips still tingled from their kiss. His children were happily dreaming in their beds. All was well with the world.

He didn't want to get hurt. But maybe, just maybe, he could take the rest of the night to be happy. To be calm. Just one night.

But even as he dozed off on the couch, he was already wishing for another day just like this one.

Chapter Eight

Mia woke up to sun streaming through the window of the guest room and a smile spreading across her face.

She'd dreamt of Linc last night. Not surprising since she'd fallen asleep thinking about his lips on hers.

It wasn't like she'd never been kissed before, but there was something about the way Linc did it that made her toes curl in pleasure. She felt like a teenager experiencing her first kiss. Not a woman in her late twenties who had already been both married and divorced.

She pushed the covers back and got out of bed. Crossing the guestroom, she glanced at herself in the mirror over the dresser, and could only shake her head. "Get it together, Mia," she said to her reflection. The big smile was still in place and her eyes were practically sparkling.

She started the new year with a plan and that plan had not included getting involved with anyone, let alone a single dad who just happened to own the company where she was working. Of course, she'd never had a plan to get divorced either, but here she was.

Still, she'd meant what she'd said to Linc the night before. The last thing she wanted to do was complicate his life. Or hers, for that matter.

Dating Linc wouldn't be easy. Not with the kids. Not with work.

She returned to bed and sank bank into the pillows and pulled the covers over her again. She snatched her phone from the bedside table where it had been charging overnight. She opened her notes app and pulled up the list she'd made on New Year's Day. Scrolling through it, she knew what she would find. Or rather, what she wouldn't: Dating. This was supposed to be her time. She was barely divorced.

She groaned out loud. To distract herself, she opened Facebook. Surely someone had posted something that would take her mind off Linc.

But any hopes of diversion were squashed when she read the reminder that today was her ex-husband's birthday. She double-checked the date on her phone.

"Of course."

Charlie was thirty-three today. She wondered if she should wish him a happy birthday. Did divorced couples do that? She had no idea. Someone should really write a manual.

Irritated, she tossed her phone to the side. She might as well go downstairs and get a cup of coffee. No use sticking around here and wallowing.

But the whole time her coffee brewed in Linc's fancy coffee maker, she stewed over her ex. She didn't realize she was grumbling out loud until Linc made his way into the kitchen.

"Something you want to share with the class?" he asked, amusement in his voice.

"No. Yes. I don't know. I mean, it's dumb."

He gave her a quizzical look. "Doesn't seem dumb if it has you this worked up."

"I...hey, look at you."

She'd just noticed that Linc was only using one crutch. He grinned.

"Seems like all this TLC is working. I appear to be mending."

"Oh my god, that's awesome."

"It is, but it doesn't get you off the hook."

She tilted her head in question.

"Mumbling, scrunched-up face, lost in thought. What's going on?"

"Oh." Mia deflated. She started a cup of coffee for Linc before taking her own to the island and sitting down. "It's stupid. Today is Charlie's birthday." Linc seemed confused. "My ex-husband," she explained.

"Ah," he said.

"I don't know if I should call him or send him a message. I mean, we were married after all. But, that's over now."

Linc nodded. "It's a tough situation. The first year is rough. All the holidays and birthdays and dates that have meaning to you. But the good news is that with each month it gets easier."

"Is that how it was with you and your ex?" she asked. As soon as the words left her mouth, she regretted them. Linc

144

turned to fix his coffee, a clear sign he still didn't want to talk about his ex-wife.

"I'm sorry, Linc."

He turned back to face her. "It's okay. Let's just say that I never even considered sending my ex a happy birthday message."

"That bad, huh?" she asked. But before he could answer the kids ran into the kitchen.

"We're up," Hadley announced.

"I can see that," Mia said. "Who's hungry?"

"Me! Me!"

She laughed as she crossed to the pantry. "Who wants cereal?"

Mia poured two bowls of cereal as Linc got the kids set up in the family room. He explained that Sundays were their special day to eat their breakfast and watch TV. Mia loved how excited kids could get over the little things.

After Hadley and Hugo were quietly eating and watching *Paw Patrol*, Mia and Linc returned to their now cold coffees. Mia quickly heated them up. She sat at the kitchen table, but Linc remained standing. She saw that he was gingerly moving his ankle back and forth.

"What should we do about dinner tonight?" she asked.

Linc thought about it. "How about chili? That's a crowd favorite around here. Plus, chili is one of those things you can make a ton of, eat some now and freeze the rest for later."

Mia loved chili but she'd never made it. She tried to think if she'd ever seen her ex eat it. Charlie wasn't really a chili-eating type of guy. Or the homemade meal type. In fact, they'd eaten out more than she felt comfortable sharing with anyone.

"I've never actually made chili," she admitted to Linc.

"You really can't mess up chili. Trust me."

Mia was fairly certain if she put her mind to it, she could ruin just about any meal out there. Including spaghetti, instant rice, and soup out of a can. Because she had already made mushy pasta, burned sauce, and she didn't even want to think about that tuna salad from last week.

"Well..." she hedged.

"Mia, this is not like getting through an encrypted firewall."

"Huh?"

Linc grinned. "It's not rocket science."

"Oh."

He grabbed a notepad that was stuck to the refrigerator with a magnet and then made his way to the table to write a list. Pausing a few times to consider, Linc finally finished the list. He handed it to her.

Mia scanned the contents. Beans, onions, ground beef, she began to read. Okay, this didn't seem too bad.

"Take my list to the grocery store. You understand what all of the ingredients are and which aisles to find them in, right?"

She nodded.

"Bring them home and I will personally walk you through each step to one of the easiest recipes on the planet. You literally dump everything into one pot."

"Can I go with you?" Hugo asked shyly from the doorway.

Mia and Linc both turned toward him. Mia wondered how long Hugo had been standing there.

"You want to go to the grocery store with Ms. Mia?" Linc asked.

Hugo nodded. "I can help Ms. Mia get the 'gredients for the chili."

"Me too, me too." Hadley ran into the room, practically knocking her brother over. "I want to go shopping too."

A little company would be nice. "Sure," Mia said enthusiastically.

Linc made a face. The way he scrunched his nose would have been adorable if she didn't get the distinct impression he was not happy about his children going to the grocery store with her.

"What?" she asked.

"Have you ever shopped with a four-year-old before?"

"No, but…"

His eyebrow arched. "How about two four-year-olds?"

She sighed. "Linc, honestly. It won't be that bad."

"Yeah," Hadley said. "It won't be that bad," she parroted.

"How about two four-year-old monsters?" Linc said, winking at his daughter.

"I think I can handle the monsters," she said confidently.

Linc grimaced. "Seriously, Mia, a trip that would definitely take less than an hour just became a whole afternoon event."

She rolled her eyes. "Honestly, it's just a little trip to the local Giant. How hard could that be?"

Linc tucked his tongue in his cheek and handed over the car keys. She thought she detected a knowing look in his eyes.

***

An hour later Mia wanted to eat her earlier words. Hadley and Hugo were a handful when they were together. Even when they weren't fighting or asking for something, they were two huge bundles of energy, who took all of her strength to corral and focus on.

And they weren't even in the grocery store yet.

But they had parked. A small success in the crowded lot. They exited the car and she grabbed each of their hands.

"We're always supposed to be with a grown-up in the parking lot," Hugo informed her.

"That's right. You don't want to get hurt or lost."

"One time Hugo got lost when we went to Costco," Hadley said. "Daddy turned white. I thought he was gonna start crying."

"It was probably a very scary moment for him."

"Then he hugged Hugo really, really tight when we found him. Then Hugo had to go to time out for running away when we got home."

"Did not," Hugo said, indignity coating his words.

"Did too," Hadley said hotly.

"You know what?" Mia said, trying to divert their attention. "I'm going to need both of your help today."

Her statement worked like a charm. Two sets of intrigued eyes flicked up to meet hers.

"You need our help?" Hugo asked.

"Yep. I'm not a very good cook," Mia said as they walked through the lot.

"We know," Hadley said.

Mia would have laughed but she felt a bit deflated by the comment. She'd always believed kids were the most honest creatures on the face of the planet. But hearing Hadley's truth about her lack of cooking skills stung.

"Right, so, I will need your help making sure that I get all of the correct groceries."

"We can definitely help with that. Right, Hugo?"

Hugo nodded.

"Great. Your dad wrote out a list, so we just have to make sure we get everything on it."

"Then you're going to cook?" Hadley asked with a sigh.

"Um, well, your dad is going to instruct me."

"Yay!"

Thanks for the support, she thought.

"What is that?" Hadley asked.

The grocery store was in the middle of a shopping complex that also contained a home renovation store, a couple clothing shops, an athletic store, a coffeehouse, and a pet store at the very end. Mia could tell from the entrance to the grocery store that something was happening down at the pet store.

"I think it might be one of those pet adoption events." She looked down at her two helpers and realized quickly they didn't understand. "Sometimes, pet stores hold events where people can come and look at animals who need families. If they find an animal they like, they can adopt it and take it home."

Instantly, both twins' eyes lit up. Uh-oh.

"Okay, let's go into the grocery store."

But Hadley and Hugo didn't budge.

"Can't we go and see the pets?" Hadley asked.

"Well, I don't know…"

"Daddy would let us look at the pets," Hadley said with an angelic smile.

"Yep, he would," Hugo added. "Daddy loves pets."

Were they teaming up on her? "He does?" If that was the case, it was strange he didn't have a cat or a dog, she thought. In any case, what would the harm be in taking the kids down to see the pets.

"I guess it wouldn't really hurt anything to go look at the pets. Right?"

***

Two hours later and Mia was once again regretting her words. She pulled into Linc's driveway, turned off the car, and swiveled in her seat to take in Hugo and Hadley, the reusable grocery bags with all of Linc's ingredients, and, oh yeah, the two kittens, being cuddled by the twins.

Mia raised her finger to her lips and started biting on her nail, recent manicure be damned. "Are you sure your dad won't be mad about the kittens?"

"Nope," Hadley said, petting the soft gray and white fur of her new pet.

"Nah," Hugo agreed. "Look, Chase just licked me."

"That means he likes you," Hadley said wisely. "My cat is purring. Do you hear her, Ms. Mia?"

"I do." The kittens really were cute. Mia had a soft spot for animals, especially cats. And she loved the fact that she was able to rescue siblings. They could stay together now. The question was, would she be able to stay at her job once Linc saw what she'd done? Could she get fired for rescuing kittens? She'd read the employee handbook on her first day. There definitely wasn't anything she remembered about animal rescue in it. Of course, there also wasn't anything about shacking up with your boss for a couple days either.

Linc appeared in the doorway to the house wearing a big grin. He was supporting himself on one crutch. Mia unbuckled her seatbelt and opened the door.

"Finally. I was getting worried about you guys. Which grocery store did you go to? One in Canada?"

"Um, well, actually…"

"Did you find all the ingredients?" he called as the twins began to climb out of their car seats.

"I did, but I kinda got some extra stuff."

"Always happens to me when I go shopping. I go in for milk and come out with a whole shopping cart of stuff I don't need."

"Yeah, but I think you might be a little surprised—"

"Ms. Mia got us kittens, Daddy."

Linc froze in the doorway at Hadley's statement. Unaware of the tension, the twins rushed to show their dad their new pets. Since Mia had never seen this particularly concerned expression on Linc's face before, she decided it would be better if she hung back and unloaded the groceries and all the pet supplies from the car. If she happened to take her time lifting each bag, well, who could blame her.

The kids had been so adorable looking at all the pets at the adoption event. Mia had laughed and taken pictures, fully intending to leave pet-less. But then, one of the volunteers showed them two kittens, a brother and sister, in need of a loving home. Hugo pointed out it was just like him and his sister.

The kittens were so cute. They were gray and white, with the prettiest black streaks throughout their soft fur. With their adorable little faces and long white whiskers, Mia knew she wouldn't be able to hold out for long. Plus, they had an almost regal air about them. Until they practically melted in her lap and began purring loudly.

She knew Linc wouldn't be thrilled, but Hugo kept insisting that "Daddy loves cats." Of course, Hadley agreed. So, Mia went into the pet store and dropped her entire paycheck on cat supplies: food, beds, toys, scratching posts, you name it.

But with every stoplight and each turn on the way home, Mia felt like she was sinking lower and lower into her seat. She'd just gotten pets—plural, as in two, not one—for someone else's kids. At least, she'd also managed to get all the ingredients for chili too. Maybe that would count for something.

"Ugh," she groaned into the silence on the outside of the door. Time to face the music. She'd carried all the grocery and pet store bags from the car, up the steps and onto the stoop. She took a deep breath and opened the door.

"I have named my kitten Belle, like in Beauty and the Beast." Hadley was holding Belle and twirling around in front of Linc.

"I named my kitten Chase. Like from Paw Patrol. Isn't that a great name, Daddy?"

"Sure is, Hugo."

It seemed like Linc was putting on a brave face for the kids, but she couldn't miss how flat his voice was. If she wasn't mistaken, he was grinding his teeth.

Mia cleared her throat and all eyes turned in her direction. "I'll, uh, just take the groceries to the kitchen. Hadley, why don't you show your dad all the stuff we got for the kittens?"

And then she made her exit as quickly as possible. Again, she tried to put the groceries away as slowly as she could, but since she was going to be using most of them shortly, it didn't take long at all. Unless of course, Linc just threw her out on the spot.

Speaking of, she heard Linc's crutch. And it was heading her way.

"I got everything on your list," she said, without looking up at him.

"Everything, and more," he said dryly. He took a seat at the island and propped his crutch next to it.

"Right. Well, see, the thing is—"

Linc held up a hand to stop her. "The thing is, you bought cats for my children."

She shook her head. "I didn't buy. I rescued." That was technically true. She'd given a donation to the shelter.

"Mia." His voice held a reprimanding tone that she'd heard him use with the twins. "You got my children cats," he repeated. "Living, breathing creatures that need love and attention. Do you have any idea how much work a pet is?"

"Of course, but the kids said—"

"They would say anything to get their way. They're four years old. You know what happens with four-year-olds?"

She gulped and shook her head.

"They have the attention span of a turnip. In three minutes, they will be on to the next thing that piques their interest. Then I'm the one stuck with two felines."

She clutched her fingers together. "I had no idea."

"You had no *right*." His eyes had darkened.

She dropped her head. "I know, I know."

"You can't just get pets for someone else's kids. That's not how it works. You didn't even check with me. What were you thinking?" With each sentence his voice rose.

"The kids said you loved pets."

"I do love pets, but that's not the point."

"Why don't you have any pets if you love them?"

"Because I'm a single, working dad, Mia. I feel like my head is barely above water most days. Why would I voluntarily add a pet to the mix?"

"I guess I didn't really think about that. I'm so sorry, Linc."

"You go out and you take my kids and you get them two cats. Then you come back here and dump them on me. Me, who's on crutches. Thanks to you. Let's not forget that I sprained my ankle because of your salsa class."

She didn't think she could feel any worse.

"What am I supposed to do now?" he asked.

"I mean, I guess if you really don't like them, you can take the kittens back."

He blew out a breath. "And break my kids' hearts. Then I'm the bad guy. Because I'm always the bad guy."

What did that mean? From what she'd seen, Hadley and Hugo idolized their father.

She opened her mouth to say something, anything, but Linc cut her off.

"God, this is just like Chrissy. You come in and you rile everything up. Guess what's going to happen in a day or two? You leave. Where does that leave me?"

154

Whoa. Mia realized nothing about this conversation was actually about her. It was Linc's past and who she assumed was his ex-wife.

"This must be great for you," Linc continued. "You get to come here and play house for a couple days. You take Hadley out for the day, which was great. But what about next weekend? And the one after that? Where will you be?"

"Linc—"

"Probably off doing something else from your list. Flitting from one whim to another. I'm the one who has to stay here. I'm the one who is always in charge. I'm responsible. I rearrange my life so I can take care of two kids. And now two cats apparently."

Even if Mia knew what to say, she probably would have kept her mouth shut.

Linc's gaze scanned the contents for the chili. He ran a hand through his hair. "You know what? I'm sure I can manage this dinner. Why don't you just leave?"

She had to work on keeping her mouth from falling open. "Leave? Are you talking about the kitchen or this house?"

"I should have just hired a nurse." He nodded at the door. "Why don't you go continue doing something on your bucket list? I have a family to care for."

Now her back was up. Did he really think she wouldn't see this commitment through? "No," she said stubbornly. "I'm not leaving you."

"Mia, I release you."

"Too bad. I told you I was here to help and that's what I'm going to do." She held her hand up when he looked to jump in with what was probably more terse words. "I messed up today.

I get that. Really, I do," she added at his skeptical face. "But let me start making it up to you."

"I really want you to leave."

"Well…we don't always get what we want. I'm staying."

Hadley ran into the kitchen, toting Belle in her arms. "Belle just licked my nose, Daddy. It was so cute." The little girl looked between the two of them. "What's going on?"

Mia took a step back. She didn't have a clue what she was supposed to say.

Linc cleared his throat. "Nothing, sweetie. Ms. Mia was just getting ready to go back to her house."

Hadley's eyes widened and her lower lip trembled. "Why?"

Mia couldn't believe he'd just said that. How dare he upset his daughter. And for no reason. So, she got them cats. Deal with it. At least, that's what she wanted to say. Instead, she would just fight his stubbornness with her own.

"You daddy's just kidding, Had. I'm not going anywhere." She pinned Linc with a very marked "go-ahead-I-dare-you" look. "You dad is going to rest that ankle now. Can you grab his ice pack?"

Relieved, Hadley ran to the freezer and retrieved the ice pack. She handed it to her dad.

"I'm going to start this dinner," Mia announced defiantly.

"You don't know how to make chili," Linc said, frost in his voice.

"I'll call my mom. Go rest. I'll be here." She turned and began sorting through the different ingredients. "Right here. Just like I said I would be."

Chapter Ten

Shockingly, Mia's chili turned out to be excellent. Just the right amount of spice.

So was Mia, he'd found out.

It had been a tense dinner. Luckily, the kids hadn't seemed to notice. They were way too excited about their new kittens.

Mia regaled them with stories of a cat named Miss Tuftsy that she'd had growing up. As she chatted away with the kids, she was all smiles and laughter. But any time she had to say anything to Linc, it was as if a switch had been flipped and the lights went out. He'd never been scared by such mundane sentences before.

Pass the salt.

I can get you more water.

There's butter for the cornbread.

Of course, she wouldn't let him get anywhere near the sink when it was time to clean up. Fine by him. Linc didn't care for doing dishes anyway.

It shouldn't bother him that Mia was clearly ticked at him. It really shouldn't. She was the one who's started all of this anyway. Everything had been going really well until she went out and got two cats.

Even if they were really adorable kittens. Linc couldn't help but smile. While Mia had been busy banging every pot and pan in the kitchen—probably on purpose too—he'd taken some time to get acquainted with his new family members.

Hugo's cat Chase was a big ball of furry fun. He was a happy cat who seemed to like to meow and bat around strings and other cat toys.

Now, Belle, was interesting. She reminded Linc of his daughter. She was the sassier of the two cats. The perfect pairing. Of course, when no one was looking, she'd climbed right into his lap, ready to be loved on. He'd stroked her soft fur and elicited the biggest purrs out of her. Just like Hadley, who never passed up an opportunity to snuggle.

He could hear Mia cleaning up the kitchen now. He wanted to go in there, but he wasn't sure what to say. He was still so angry about the cats. About her presumptuousness.

He shook his head. Hours later, and he still needed to cool down before talking to her again.

Even though it was torture going up the stairs on his crutches, Linc wanted to check and make sure everyone was tucked in. What he saw when he finally climbed the stairs had his heart melting.

Both of his kids were in their respective beds, cuddling with their new kittens. It was the most adorable sight he'd ever seen.

He leaned against the doorframe of Hadley's pink and purple room. Her little crystal lamp was on, just the way she liked it. The soft light illuminated his sweet, and bubbly, daughter tucked into a mass of ruffles and pillows. Belle was curled up in a little ball right on Hadley's pillow. The two seemed to be breathing in sync. Linc couldn't help it. He whipped out his phone and snapped a picture.

Then he hobbled over to his son's room. In complete contrast to Hadley's frilly, girly bedroom decor, Hugo's room was decorated in a sea of dark blue with a plethora of trains and cars. Chase was sprawled on Hugo's chest and his boy had a peaceful smile on his sleeping face. Again, Linc snapped a picture.

As he made his way back down to the first floor, he considered the events of the day. He hobbled by a bevy of cat toys. Mia must have spent a fortune on all the cat paraphernalia. Now that he thought about it, they had food and water dishes, toys, scratching posts, litter boxes, and more. She didn't have to do that.

Of course, if she hadn't gotten the cats in the first place….

But there was something else. Something he couldn't deny. Mia's resolve to stay in the house was impressive. He'd been laying into her pretty harshly, but she honored her commitment to not only him, but to the kids.

Something Chrissy never did.

"Damn," he grumbled to himself as he continued to carefully make his way down the stairs.

He'd been comparing Mia and Chrissy all day. How many other things in his life did he hold up to the low standard Chrissy set?

If he was being honest, Linc could see Chrissy doing the same thing, getting pets on a whim. Only, she wouldn't have followed through the way Mia had. There would be no cat toys or kitty litter. Buying food for the kittens wouldn't have even crossed her mind.

That said nothing of sticking around after a blowup. How many fights had ended with Chrissy bailing and Linc sticking around to pick up the pieces?

Mia had stayed.

His anger began dissipating. Not disappearing completely. Nope, some of it lingered. But he did need to make things right with Mia.

He found her in the family room, staring at the television. The remote was in her hand and her arm was propped on her knees. She kept changing the channel.

"Listen, Linc," she said by way of greeting. She didn't even look up from the TV.

"Hey," he said, sinking into an armchair. He propped his leg on the matching ottoman.

She sighed. "I get that your angry with me. I really, really understand it. I overstepped a huge boundary."

"Yes, you did."

She continued to stare straight ahead at the changing channels. "It was a mistake and I'm sorry." With a flourish, she punched a button on the remote and the TV turned off. She swiveled to face him. "But kicking me out of your house was completely uncalled for."

"Yes, it was."

"Furthermore...wait, what?"

He let out a small laugh. How could he not at the quizzical look on her face.

Linc leaned forward. "I didn't actually kick you out of the house because you wouldn't leave." He waited, but she didn't laugh at his lame joke. "I did try to kick you out though, and for that, I'm very sorry."

"Oh."

Yeah, oh. "I may have overreacted a tad," he admitted.

Her eyes narrowed, but she remained silent.

"I know how persuasive my children can be," he continued. "Especially when they join forces. It's hard enough to resist one of them. But the pair is damn near impossible."

"Are you still mad?"

Was he? Linc considered the question. She'd gotten them two cats. It could have been worse. Cats were definitely easier than dogs. Imagine having to train two puppies. But they were more work than two goldfish. Or pet rocks.

"Do you still want me to leave?" she asked without waiting for him to answer her first question.

"No." He was able to answer quickly and easily. He liked having her in his house. He liked watching her interact with his children. Maybe that was part of the problem he was having.

She was also helping him. The kids had school the next day and Mia would be dropping them off. She was even going to pick them up and return them home, before she went back to work. Hadley had a ballet lesson to get to and Hugo had a play-date with Josh.

Not to mention, she would be preparing dinner and helping with bath time.

He didn't just like having her at the house. He needed her.

And that was the root of the next problem. Needing someone.

"I want you to stay the next couple of days. In fact, I'd really appreciate the help."

Linc leaned even further and reached for her hand. Unfortunately, he wouldn't be able to touch her unless he got up, which would involve using his crutch.

Luckily, Mia closed the distance and clasped her hand with his.

"I am sorry, Linc. I wasn't thinking and I got caught up in the moment."

"Like I said, I know how the kids can be when they want something." He squeezed her fingers. "I'm sorry too. I shouldn't have blown up like that. It's been an emotional time around here."

"Injuries always bring out extra emotions," she said, nodding.

"It's not that," he admitted.

She sat back against the couch. "You said something earlier."

He felt embarrassed. He'd really laid into her when she'd first gotten back from the store. "I said a lot of things earlier."

She shook her head. "Something about always being the bad guy."

He nodded. Of course, she would be interested in that comment. He didn't really want to explain, because explaining would

162

mean delving into his time with his ex. He would have to share what really happened between him and Chrissy and why she wasn't around now. But since Mia had told him about her marriage, he imagined he should share what had gone down in his.

"Would you like something to drink?" he asked.

"Are you stalling?" she asked.

"Absolutely. But I feel like this will be easier with alcohol."

"Many things are." She laughed. "Sure, I'd love some red wine. Here, let me get it. What would you like?"

"A beer would be great." Hopefully the cold liquid would coat his dry throat and help him get the words out easier.

She went to the kitchen, and he could hear her opening the cabinet and then the fridge. He heard liquid being poured. Then she returned to the living room and handed him a cold mug of beer. She took a sip of her wine, her tongue darting out to lick her lips. Then she tucked her legs underneath her and sat back, clearly anticipating his story.

Linc wasn't quite sure where to start. "I was married."

"Yes, you were."

He took a long pull of beer. "This is hard."

She reached for his hand and covered it with hers. Her skin was so soft and smooth. "Linc, I understand. I really, really do."

Of course, she did.

"My wife, my ex-wife, that is, was pure chaos. When we were dating, that unpredictability and spontaneity was wonderful. It was exciting. Probably what attracted me to her. Because I've never been like that. I was always the guy with a plan."

He swallowed more beer. "With Chrissy, I got to be someone else, someone fun. For a while, I didn't have to worry much about deadlines or schedules."

"Mm," Mia said, her face turning thoughtful. "That can be freeing. For a time."

"Chrissy would pick up and go at the drop of a hat. She'd wake me up in the middle of the night and drag me out to look at the stars. We would put everything aside and run off for weekend trips."

"Sounds nice."

"It was fun. Then the twins came. They were, uh, kinda, well…"

"Unexpected?" she finished for him.

"A definite surprise. A wonderful, amazing surprise." He paused for a long moment. "At least, they were for me."

"Ah," she said. In that short little word, there was so much understanding.

"Chrissy wasn't happy. She tried to play it off. But I could tell."

Mia worried her lip. He could tell she wanted to ask something but wasn't sure if she should. "Go ahead and ask it," Linc said.

"What aspect was she not happy about? When she found out she was pregnant, or was the timing in general off?"

"The timing would have never been right."

Mia met his eyes. She waited patiently.

"Children cramped Chrissy's style. She was used to doing whatever she wanted whenever the mood struck her. Having two kids took that freedom away from her."

"Some people aren't meant to be parents," Mia said.

His mom had said the same thing to him. Many times. "I know that rationally, but…"

"It's hard to be rational about something as important as children. I get it."

"Do you?" Linc ran a hand over his face. He hated the way he felt whenever he talked about Chrissy. A sinking feeling took over and suddenly he was moody and angsty.

He wanted to pace, but his ankle denied him that option. "I don't know if I will ever be able to get my head around the fact that Chrissy disappeared. I mean, she flat out went away. Well, actually, she did come back for a few months claiming she was sorry and told me she was back for good."

"What happened?" Mia asked.

"The same thing that happened every time with her. She only stayed with us for a couple months. She got that urge to flee and off she went again. And after, I mean, I thought…"

"After what?"

"After she went through this whole song and dance about making a mistake. She told me she wanted to try and be a mother and wife. I wasn't even suspicious. Not in the slightest bit. I thought that maybe after she had the twins, she'd experienced some postpartum depression. That could account for why she left."

"You never know, Linc. Maybe that's true and she's still going through it."

He shook his head. "Chrissy wasn't able to find a doctor who would back that story up in court. In the end, after what felt like forever, she signed all parental responsibilities to me. She has no desire to be around her own children."

Mia sat back, chewing on a fingernail.

"What are you thinking?" He could tell she was deep in thought.

"I don't think this is only about Hugo and Hadley."

"What do you mean?"

She scooted forward on the couch. Her knees were almost touching his. "Everything you've said so far has centered around the kids. But you loved her, Linc, and she hurt you. She left you too."

"I, well…" Damn, he wanted to stand. He wanted to be anywhere but here.

"I can't imagine how you must have felt when she came back for those few months."

How had it felt? Linc didn't usually think about it. In fact, he actively blocked remembering. But now that Mia brought it up, those walls he'd built around it started to tumble. He knew exactly how he'd felt. Happy. Relieved.

"I loved her, and I was thrilled she came back," he said in a soft voice.

Mia nodded. She covered his hand with hers. "Of course, you were."

"I forgave everything. Everything." His voice rose the second time he said *everything*. But he quickly remembered the children were sleeping upstairs and lowered his voice again. "For a few months, we were a real family. She seemed happy."

Happy, but not content. Linc could tell. Only, he didn't want to admit that. Not to anyone, and most definitely not to himself.

Mia squeezed his hand. "Obviously, she wasn't."

"When the twins were born, a lot was going on in our lives. It was such a busy time. My company was flourishing. My partner and I were swamped hiring new employees, just trying to keep up. We were growing faster than we ever dreamed. Then the offers started pouring in."

"Offers?"

"To buy the company. We had to sort through all that. It was a lot of overtime, a lot of meetings with lawyers. All good problems to have."

"But it couldn't have been easy with a wife and two new babies."

Understatement. "It wasn't." He closed his eyes remembering the limited sleep, the stress, the uncertainty. "Still, I wanted…" He paused, wondering what Mia would think. He knew how Chrissy had reacted.

"What?" Mia asked. "You wanted more time? Help?"

"More kids."

"Oh."

Yeah, oh.

"How did Chrissy feel about that?"

"She wasn't happy. She wouldn't even entertain the thought really." And she stopped letting him touch her after that. "I think the minute I mentioned the desire for more children, it was her breaking point. That's when she decided to move on.

"But, dammit." He slammed his hand on the arm of the chair. "I was upfront about wanting a big family from the very beginning. Even back when we were in college and just dating.

I'm an only child. I wanted my kids to have lots of siblings. I wanted more kids…"

"Still do?" she asked softly.

He pushed a hand through his hair. "How crazy is that?"

She smiled kindly. "There's nothing crazy about expressing your desires. It's odder to me when people don't reveal what they really want. When they keep it hidden. Which is kind of what Chrissy did."

He nodded glumly. "One morning, she was gone. Just up and left in the middle of the night, I guess."

"Oh, Linc." She moved to sit on the ottoman in front of him, careful not to jar his ankle.

"To make matters worse, eventually I began to acclimate to life without her. Again. It was my parents urging that I file for divorce."

"You have to move on."

"But I never saw the custody fight coming. Why would she want to fight for custody when she walked out on her children twice?"

"Why did she?"

He glanced at the stairs again. Sometimes Hadley woke up at night and would tiptoe down the stairs unbeknownst to him for who knew how long. He had to make sure sensitive ears weren't listening. No matter what, he wouldn't tarnish their mother in front of them.

"Chrissy has a mean streak. I've already described her as childish. But she can also be vindictive and cold."

"Like those kids who break toys. If they can't have it, no one can."

He pointed at her. "Exactly."

She patted his leg. "Have you thought about talking to a counselor or psychologist?"

"Oh yeah. The kids have seen someone."

She shook her head slowly. "No, Linc. Not just the kids. You."

"Huh?"

"This, all the stuff Chrissy did to you and your family, wasn't about you. You get that right?"

He shrugged. "After she left the second time, I moved us from California back here to the East. I thought the change in scenery would be good for the kids."

"And for you," Mia said knowingly. "From what you're telling me, it sounds like Chrissy wasn't thinking about you at all. Or the kids. Only herself and what she wanted and needed in that moment. It's not fair to you, but it's not about you either."

"How do I ever trust someone again? Really truly commit myself to another person. Will they do the same thing?"

"Trust issues," she said on a sigh. "I know about those."

Of course, she did. He offered a small smile. "The hardest part is that it's not only me anymore. I have two little ones to think about. And they're getting older. They understand more. They see more. I can't put them through that. Not again. The questions about their mother have been increasing lately."

She leaned toward him. For a moment, Linc thought she would press her lips to his. Instead, she looked deeply into his eyes. It was almost as if she was searching for something.

"You're a good man, Linc. But you can't let Chrissy's actions define your life."

Mia hadn't let her ex-husband guide her life. In fact, quite the opposite. She went from being Amelia Dewitt to Mia Reynolds. She was doing things every day that she'd always wanted to do. It was actually inspiring.

He closed the distance between them with a tender kiss. He tried to pour himself into the kiss; desperately wanting Mia to realize that it meant so much to him that she listened to him tonight, that she was helping with his children, that she didn't leave today.

Maybe he could be with Mia without getting hurt.

The kiss ended. Mia smiled and patted his cheek. "I'm glad you told me about Chrissy."

He'd handed her power by revealing his past life. She knew the way to destroy him. Linc searched her eyes, scouring the depths of that pretty blue. He didn't think she would do the same thing to him as Chrissy.

Just as he was about to let himself fully go, something caught his attention out of the corner of his eye. Hugo's cat crept around the corner, scratching his body along the wall.

The cats that Mia had spontaneously gotten that day. Impulsive. Like Chrissy.

Chapter Eleven

"How was playing house?"

Mia refused to acknowledge her sister's question. Putting a hand to her ear, she pretended that the background noise from the bar was too loud for her to hear.

Emerson laughed. "Fine. Ignore me. I'll be here all night."

Before she could respond, Grace arrived in her usual flurry. She was wearing a gorgeous, tailored black pant suit that accentuated all of her lush curves. She'd accessorized with large emerald-colored jewelry that matched her eyes perfectly.

The three of them had decided to meet for happy hour to catch up and discuss Grace's wedding. Although, Mia knew Grace had been planning her wedding since the age of three.

They were sitting at a high table in the newest trendy bar on Alexandria's waterfront, only a few blocks from Mia's office. Mia liked the décor. It had an old farmhouse feel to it with vaulted ceilings with large wooden beams, stone accent walls and tables made of reclaimed wood. The lighting was kept low, with candles everywhere and large windows that let in the light from passing boats in the marina.

A waiter appeared, detailing the happy hour specials. Mia and Grace both ordered glasses of red wine, Emerson went with scotch on the rocks, and they decided to split a plate of calamari to start.

After settling in and hearing about the meeting Grace just came from, both Emerson and Grace faced her with expectant expressions.

"What?" she asked.

"So?" Emerson raised a brow in question.

"So what?" Mia shifted to allow the waiter to place their drinks on the table. Thank god the liquid had arrived. Mia had a feeling she'd need to keep her throat nice and wet.

"You just moved in with your boss and his kids," Emerson said.

Grace leaned forward. "We're dying to hear how it went."

Mia took a sip of wine. "It was fine."

"Fine?" That's it? I talked to mom and she told me that you brought Linc's daughter into the store. She was a big hit."

Mia's shoulders relaxed. "She really was. It was so adorable. Mom let Hadley try on flower girl dresses and veils and tiaras. I have pictures." She whipped out her phone and pulled up Hadley's photo shoot.

"And you weren't playing house?" Emerson asked.

"Hush," Grace said. "I love this." She tasted her wine as she perused Mia's photos. "So, you got along with the kids?"

"Oh yeah. Hadley and Hugo are amazing. They're both adorable. Hugo is shyer than his sister. But he's just the sweetest. He idolizes his dad. You can just see it every time he looks at Linc. And Hadley, OMG, she's going to be a handful, for sure. She's all girly princess, but with this inherent sass."

"Uh-huh."

"What?" she asked her sister.

"What about Linc?" Emerson asked.

"What about him?"

"Come on, Mia," Grace said. "You spent almost an entire week living with him. How did it go? Did any romantic fireworks go off?"

"Oh, jeez, Gracie." Emerson rolled her eyes. "The last thing Mia needs is for fireworks to go off with her boss. Or anyone. She's on a journey to be her own independent woman."

Mia slouched in her chair. She could feel her nose scrunching up.

"Right, Mia?" Emerson asked, concern lacing her voice. "You're still being an independent woman?"

"I mean…," Mia began.

Grace held her wine glass in the air. "Wait a minute. She can be both independent and strong and still have romance in her life." Grace pointed the glass at Emerson. "You did. So did I."

"I know that. But neither of us had recently left a bad marriage. She's still healing."

"She's stronger than you think," Grace countered.

"*She* is still right here at this very table," Mia said. "Em, I love you, but you worry about me too much. I think Grace is right." At least, she hoped Grace was on point with her assessment that a woman could be both independent and romantic at the same time.

"Everything went well while I stayed with Linc."

While they feasted on the calamari that had just been delivered, she filled them in on the dinners she made, or attempted to make. They all laughed at her attempt at making ziti. Then she told them about the cats.

"You got Linc's kids a couple of cats?" Grace asked shoving a piece of the breaded fish in her mouth.

"Oh, Mia." Emerson shook her head. "That's a huge responsibility."

Feeling defensive, she pointed at her sister. "You have Cosmo."

"Not the same thing," Emerson said. "Jack inherited his father's dog. And there are two of us and one dog. One dog who is fully trained. Still, we can barely keep up some days. Cosmo definitely rules the house. And he's a ton of work."

There really wasn't any way to defend her decision with the cats. She knew it. "Yeah, it wasn't my finest moment."

"Was Linc mad?" Grace asked.

"Oh yeah. We really had it out."

"So, I guess no romance after all," Grace said, sighing heavily.

"Um, actually…"

"Wait, what?" Emerson said.

"No!" Grace sat forward excitedly.

"We've kissed," Mia admitted. "A couple times."

"Before the cat incident or after?" Emerson wanted to know.

"Um, both. But more before than after."

"You kissed?" Grace squealed. "Oh my god, this is amazing. You and Linc. Linc and you. I mean, I've only met him at a couple industry events, but he's such a cutie. And so smart. And from what you've told us, a really great dad. That's important."

Mia couldn't help but laugh at Grace's enthusiasm. Even before Grace became engaged, she was in love with love and wanted everyone she knew to be in love and happy too.

Still, Mia couldn't help but notice her sister's reaction. Or, non-reaction, as the case may be. Emerson's lips were locked tight. She was watching Mia and her best friend but staying mum.

"Well, Em? Say something."

"You're making a mistake."

The waiter stopped by the table again and eyed their almost empty glasses. "Another round?"

"Oh yeah," Grace answered for all of them as her eyes darted between Mia and her sister.

Emerson reached across the table and squeezed Mia's hand. "I'm not trying to rain on your parade. I promise. I do worry about you. Probably too much, but I'm your big sister and that's never going to change."

Mia let out a breath she hadn't been aware she was holding. "I kinda love that about you."

"But I do want to point out that Linc is your boss at work."

"It's not unheard of for coworkers to date," Grace stated.

"It's also tough when the relationship doesn't work out. And there are only three people in her office." Emerson took the last sip of her scotch. "Plus, he's a single dad. That can't be easy."

"I think he handles everything extremely well," Mia said defensively.

Emerson held up a hand. "All I'm saying is that you need to tread lightly. Whatever is happening between the two of you needs to be given careful thought. This can't be a one-night stand or a superficial relationship. There better be real feelings behind it. It's time to get serious."

Mia began to chew on a nail until she remembered her recent manicure. "We're both being serious. In fact, Linc told me about his ex-wife." Mia glanced down at the table. "There are issues there. Big issues."

"Another reason to stop this now," Emerson said.

"Issues can be worked on and worked through," Grace said diplomatically.

Mia knew Grace had worked through a lot when she and Xander were getting together. It hadn't been easy, but they were one of the best couples she'd ever seen.

"You want my advice?" Emerson asked.

Mia sat up straight in her chair. "Yes, of course."

"In your marriage, you lost *you*. I don't want that to happen again."

"It won't, Em. I promise."

Emerson held up her hand. "You can't know that for sure. My advice to you is to put a stop to this now. Go back to focusing on you. Learning who you are and what you want before you enter a relationship again. Concentrate on your job."

Maybe it was all the comments she used to receive doing pageants and dance competitions, but Mia usually enjoyed getting advice. She liked to sort through it and find useful things to help her grow as a person.

Unfortunately, the problem here was that she'd just been given really good advice. Advice she knew would be practically impossible to take.

***

By the end of the week, Linc was gingerly walking on his ankle. He'd returned to his doctor, who said his ankle was healing just fine.

His heart? That was another matter entirely.

It had felt cathartic to share the history of his and Chrissy's relationship with Mia. She brought a fresh perspective to the situation. Still, she'd also brought a flurry of other things into his life: his children undying love, the stirring of feelings he didn't want to experience, and, of course, cats.

Not that he would share it, but Linc was actually enjoying having pets around the house. Hard to stay mad when Belle or Chase would climb up on his chest and purr. Not to mention how his heart melted every night when he tucked the kids in as their respective kittens snuggled with them. Plus, Hadley and Hugo were both intent on making sure their cats had food and water. He was impressed with how responsible they were being.

Now, the litter box. That was another story.

After their long talk about Chrissy, things had been pretty tame between him and Mia. She'd cooked a couple of good meals for the kids. Linc had worked from home but Mia had made sure Hadley and Hugo got everywhere they needed to be. No one was late and everything ran smoothly.

To be honest, it had been incredible to have another adult to rely on. Linc liked to think he was doing the best job with his kids as he could. But sharing responsibility had really made a difference. He'd actually been able to read. An entire book. Just for pleasure. It was mind-boggling how two parents in one household could really relieve the load.

Last night, however, had been a difficult one. It was Mia's last evening with them. After dinner, she returned to her townhouse. The kids didn't take it well. They'd grown very used to the pretty Ms. Mia.

So had he.

But his ankle was getting better and there was nothing holding him back from returning to his usual life. So long as he still iced his ankle a couple times a day and did the exercises the doctor recommended, he was good to go.

So why hadn't he been able to fall asleep last night? The kids were in bed. The house was quiet.

But, the house was quiet. Too quiet. He'd missed Mia.

Which he really shouldn't, because he needed to be careful with her.

"There's a man with something on his mind."

He started at Nadine's words. He was back in the office for the first time all week. He thought coming in on a Friday would be good. Fridays were typically easier and then it would be the weekend. A nice way to ease back into his routine.

"I have a lot of things on my mind," he answered.

"Any you want to share?" Nadine propped her hip on his desk, making herself completely comfortable. As usual.

"Nothing about work."

He'd hoped that would be the end of it. But he should have known better. Nadine had other plans.

"How was your week at home?" she asked, with something akin to a twinkle in her eye.

"I injured my ankle so there was a lot of pain and icing and anti-inflammatories."

Nadine whooshed a hand in front of his face, the way one might swat a pesky fly. "Stop being so dramatic. It was just a sprain."

"Thank you for your sympathy."

"My pleasure. Now, what about Mia?"

Linc shot a glance in the direction of her cubicle. But she wasn't there. She'd run out to meet her mother for lunch. She should be back any minute now....

"What about Mia?" he asked.

"I'm not saying a word," Nadine said, with a sly expression on her face.

"And yet, you just said plenty of them," Linc countered.

"What? I think it's great that you asked Mia to help you out. You're far too stubborn. It was nice to see you let someone in."

"I didn't ask her. She volunteered." Or had he asked her? Linc couldn't quite remember. That night in the hospital had been a blur. After all, that had been their first kiss. Between the hurt in his foot and the happiness in his heart, he'd been a bit vulnerable.

The front door opened, and Mia flitted in. Even though it was a dark, cloudy day, her entrance seemed to bring the light. She waved to them with a big grin. As she began to remove her scarf and coat, the main phone started ringing. She plopped in her chair and went into business mode.

At her arrival, something relaxed inside him. He liked being able to look up from his desk and see her. Her presence was comforting to him.

"Earth to Linc. You still with me?" Nadine asked.

"Sorry, I was…"

"Staring at Mia?" Nadine chuckled. "Boy, I have two eyes. I see what's going on around here."

"You see nothing because there isn't anything to see. Mia is over there and I'm over here."

"And she was at your house for close to a week."

"Helping."

"Is that what we're calling it these days?"

He shot a disturbed look in Nadine's direction. But he quickly relented. "I have to admit that it was really nice to have another adult around. Someone to talk to who wasn't wearing a tutu or an Avenger's costume."

"Welcome back to the land of adults."

"It was great…." He let his words trail off.

Nadine arched a brow. "But?"

How much did he reveal? Nadine knew him better than most people. And she knew Chrissy. If anyone was qualified to talk to about this, it was Nadine.

He moved his chair to peer around Nadine at Mia. She was still busy on the phone, although she had managed to remove her coat.

He lowered his voice. "Mia has an impulsive side."

"A lot of people do," Nadine said diplomatically.

"She got the twins cats." Linc waited, but Nadine didn't flinch. "Without my permission." Still, nothing from Nadine. "She went out to get ingredients for chili and came back with two kittens."

"Ah, I bet Hadley and Hugo were over the moon about it."

"They were, but that's not the point."

"I'll have to bring over some 'welcome to the family' presents. Hm, maybe some cat toys? Or one of those big cat trees."

A cat tree? More new stuff? Where would they put that? Linc wiped his palms on his pant legs.

Nadine grabbed his shoulders, looking him right in the eyes. "Lincoln, calm down. I can see we're losing you to the questions in your head."

She really did know him too well.

All he could respond with was, "She got them cats."

Nadine nodded. "Cats are easy. Lower maintenance than dogs."

"That's not the point," he said stubbornly.

She nailed him with a no-nonsense stare. "They are also much lower maintenance than leaving you with two babies."

Touché. One point for Nadine. Still, as much as he liked the kittens, he wasn't quite ready to forget that Mia had added more responsibility to his life. "I now have two kids and two pets to look after. Because of Mia."

Nadine leaned back and hit him with one of her famous no-bullshit stares. "She also took your daughter out for the entire day. How did you like her spontaneity then?"

Yeah, that had been great. Wonderful, really. Hadley was still talking about it, and Linc had a feeling she would be for quite some time.

"One of these days I'm going to regret telling you things."

"So, you've said. I doubt it." Nadine softened. "Just so we're clear. There is a big difference between impulsiveness and recklessness."

"I know that."

"Do you? Because I was getting the impression that brilliant brain of yours was starting to compare Mia with your ex."

"They have similarities."

Nadine tilted her head. She was quiet for a moment. "They have a lot of differences too. Mia is kind and patient. She's a hard worker and she follows through with projects."

"But she doesn't know who she is yet. She's recently divorced and out there searching for herself."

Nadine shrugged. "I'm in my forties."

Linc clamped down on the urge to guffaw. He did raise an eyebrow though and let out a very distinct *ahem*.

"Fine. I'm in my fifties. I've had to go searching for myself many times over the years. Who am I? What do I want? More important, what do I need right now at this particular moment in life."

"Your point is?"

"It's natural for Mia to do the same. She doesn't realize this yet. Hell, you don't either. But I can see it. That girl knows who she is much more than she thinks."

"But…" He raised his hands and then immediately let them drop. He didn't even know what to say without sounding like a child.

"But she brought you two cats," Nadine filled in.

"Without asking."

"Oh please," Nadine swiped a hand full of glittery rings in the air. "Let me ask you this. What would you have said if she'd broached the subject of getting cats? Be honest."

"I would have said no. I don't have time for that."

"I told you to be honest."

He would have probably been taken aback in the beginning. Then, he would have thought long and hard about it. In the end, he would have agreed that the kids needed some pets around.

"Lincoln," Nadine urged.

"Fine. I would have allowed the cats to become part of the family."

Nadine grinned.

"But it was still impulsive," he couldn't help but add.

Mia appeared then and Linc almost fell off his chair. She emitted a small cough as she clutched a paper to her chest.

Nadine angled toward her. "Hey, Mia. What's that?"

"Well, I kinda did something that you might not like. I mean, it's not bad. It's just that I probably should have run it by you first."

Linc shot Nadine a look trying to convey that everything he'd just said was right. First the cats, now whatever this was.

Nadine made a big show of turning her back to him. "What is it?" she asked.

"I entered the website in a competition. I'm familiar with this contest. They have all kinds of different categories, from best marketing to best association magazine, and so much more. They're pretty reputable." She bit her lip. "They had extended the deadline for entries and...um, well...turns out we're one of the finalists for Best Up & Coming Website."

The room was silent for a moment as they let her words sink in. Best website? For Something True? Linc couldn't keep the pride from swelling in his chest.

"That's wonderful news," Nadine said, standing up. She took the paper from Mia and scanned it. "Did you hear that, Linc? Our little pet project is up for best website."

She thrust the paper forward and Linc saw that it was a list of all the finalists. "Hey, I know some of these other sites. I can't believe we're up against them. Wow."

Mia grinned and clapped her hands together. "You guys did such a fantastic job with this site."

"Now with you on board, we're unstoppable." As Nadine continued to gush, Linc quickly turned to his computer and did a search on the contest. When he found the homepage, he scanned the requirements for entry. Then he lingered on the finalists' page so he could take in Something True's name.

"I know this award. It's given by WMSM. Websites, Marketing & Social Media," he explained. "They're an association who educate small businesses about marketing and communications, and how to maximize their websites. They host a pretty well-attended conference every year."

"Right," Mia said, her eyes lighting up. "The conference leads up to the awards banquet. How did you know about it?"

"Hm?" Linc was still scanning the website. "Oh, they asked me to speak," he said absentmindedly. When he looked up from his computer, both women were staring at him.

Mia spoke first. "They wanted you to be a speaker at WMSM? That's huge, Linc."

"Why didn't you say yes?" Nadine asked at almost the same time. She exchanged a look with Mia. "That would have been great exposure for Something True."

"I don't know. The conference is in New Jersey. It's time away from the kids. Hadley has her ballet recital the week after."

Linc reread the contest qualifications again. "I can't believe they even considered us for best website. We don't have a huge following on social media yet and a lot of these other sites do."

Mia coughed. "Actually, that was the other news I wanted to share. I took your advice, Linc."

Nadine faced him with a big "oh really" stare.

"I gave Mia permission to look into our social media and marketing when she had some free time. Sorry, I forgot to mention it."

"Right. Well, I started an Instagram account and we're already up to 3,000 followers. I created a content calendar for the Facebook page, and I found that posting consistently has really helped our presence with Facebook's ever-changing algorithms. I've increased our followers by twenty percent."

"Um, wow." Nadine looked incredibly impressed. Linc knew the feeling. When he gave the green light for Mia to look into social media, he had no idea he was unleashing a social media wizard.

"Mia, that's wonderful," Nadine said. "I knew I was doing the right thing hiring you. I could feel it. You're doing such an amazing job."

Mia beamed. Linc couldn't deny that seeing her delight at being praised had his throat tightening. He wasn't only proud of her. He was proud *for* her.

Nadine continued. "I love to post pics on my own Instagram and Facebook accounts, but I would have no idea how to increase our numbers. And I would have never thought to enter the website in a competition. Would you, Linc?"

He had to admit that he wouldn't. Mia was doing excellent work. Even if she was going off on her own to do it. "Nope," he said.

These were good things. So why was he still feeling at odds with it?

Because Mia was ushering change into his life and he couldn't be sure he was ready for it. Or that he wanted it at all. Or that it was needed. First, she ushered upheaval into his personal life by bewitching his children and bestowing them with cats. Now, she was making changes at work. It was a lot to take in.

He ran a frustrated hand through his hair and tried to rationalize. Of course, they needed social media. And naturally, even being a finalist in a contest was something they could use in marketing. Let alone if they won. Something True, an award-winning website. It had a nice ring to it.

Mia was staring at him. Probably waiting for more than his simple "nope." When he failed to offer anything else, she shuffled her feet and turned to Nadine.

"Well, it was my pleasure. There's a fancy dinner for the awards at the end of the two days of the conference. But…"

"But what?" Nadine asked.

Here we go, Linc thought. There was always more than what was originally described. It had been the same with Chrissy. He couldn't imagine what else was going to go along with this conference.

"It's in Atlantic City," Mia said shyly.

Oh. That wasn't so bad.

"Right." She clasped her hands, twisting her fingers together. "It's in a month, which I know is really short notice," she said quickly. "But we get a discount on conference registrations. Of course, the awards banquet would be free since we're finalists." She finished with an expectant look in her eyes.

He realized something. This event was important to her. He could tell by the way Mia was being careful about what she said and how she said it.

"Should I sign you both up for it?" Mia asked. "I was checking out their classes and workshops and they have tracks on everything. I think there might even be some stuff for you, Linc."

If anyone should go to this thing, it should be her, of that Linc was sure of.

"You did the work. I think you should get a ticket too," Nadine said, reading his mind.

"Oh no," Mia said, twisting those hands together again. "I mean, you guys founded Something True."

"And you are helping to grow it," Linc finished. "Nadine is right. You should be the one to go. Those classes will be good for you, especially since you've apparently taken over our social media." He hadn't meant the words to sound bitter or snotty, but somehow, they had anyway. Nadine shot him a look.

"I can't imagine what you'll be able to do our social media after you take the classes,' Nadine said. "How about this? Why don't you and Linc attend the conference?"

His chest tightened. "I can't go to Atlantic City."

Nadine placed a hand on her hip. "Why not?"

"Um, hello," he said. He couldn't believe she didn't understand why he was hesitant to go to this.

"What?" Nadine asked, clueless.

"He's worried about Hadley and Hugo," Mia said.

She got it. He couldn't believe she understood. He wanted to hug her.

"Oh please," Nadine said, waving a dismissive hand. "I was just talking to your mother this morning and she was saying how much she would love a visit with the kids. She hasn't seen them since Christmas."

"I mean, I guess I could ask her…"

"Great. It's settled," Nadine said quickly.

Linc immediately started thinking of worst-case scenarios. The house could catch fire. There could be a terrorist attack. And he would be gone. In a different state. He had to offer one last-ditch effort.

"What about the office? We can't just close up shop for a couple days."

"I'll cover everything down here and meet you for the free booze and food at the end." Nadine winked.

188

"Are you sure?" Mia asked, practically crossing her fingers. She shot Linc a look. "Will you be okay, Linc?"

"The twins will be with their grandparents. They'll love it." Nadine offered a firm nod.

"Yes," Linc said, backing up Nadine. "You will get a lot out of this.

Mia clasped her hands together and grinned widely before returning to her desk. They both watched her retreating back.

"What was that?" Nadine asked sharply once Mia was out of earshot. "You actually sounded mad or irritated for a second over some really great work that our employee did on our behalf."

"On behalf of the website. And we didn't ask her to do that."

"It shows initiative," Nadine said.

"She didn't take into consideration what we, her two bosses, would say." He held up a hand when he saw that Nadine was ready to jump in. "It costs money to enter that contest too. Where did she code the invoice to?"

Nadine frowned. "I don't know. She's been handing me all the invoices and accounting information. I haven't seen anything cross my desk for this. Still, this is really fabulous news. She did good."

"She's impulsive and that kind of trait leads to chaos." He clenched his jaw. "She's added a lot to my workload. I need to add an Instagram widget on the website. I'll need to add this new info about the contest." Both of which would take him a total of two minutes to accomplish. They were weak excuses at best, and he knew it.

Nadine rolled her eyes. "Did you even hear any of that?" She pointed toward Mia. "Impulsive? Chaos? You're nuts. These are all good things. You know what else would be good?"

"I have a feeling you're going to tell me."

"You getting some time away from the kids. You need a break, Linc. Besides, our little wedding project could be winning an award. Wouldn't that be great for marketing and PR?"

He wasn't about to reveal he thought the same thing.

"See, Linc. Some surprises can actually turn out to be good."

He still wasn't sure if he agreed, but he knew he was about to find out.

Chapter Twelve

The month leading up to the conference had been a busy one. In both good and bad ways.

The website was getting more unique views than ever. Linc noticed that Mia was really working hard on social media. Posts, tweets, pics and stories were going up every day. She even wrote up a press release about their award nomination. Nadine was ecstatic. Linc had to admit that he was impressed, too.

He'd met with Nadine to discuss Mia's future at Something True. Their receptionist might just be moving into more of a communications, marketing and PR role in the coming months. Linc couldn't wait to tell her because he knew Mia would be overjoyed at the idea.

However, the month had also seen its share of downsides too. And not just because he was nervous about leaving the kids when he went to Atlantic City.

A lovely case of stomach flu worked itself through his household, starting with Hugo, moving on to Hadley, and finally settling in with Linc. Linc felt fairly confident saying that there was nothing worse in the entire world than the stomach flu. Fun times.

Mia had offered to come over and help, but Linc honestly didn't want to expose her to the germs. It was one thing to help him chauffeur the kids around when he'd sprained his ankle, but a stomach bug was no joke. After spending twenty-four hours hugging the bathroom floor, Linc could say with absolute certainty that he wouldn't wish this on his worst enemy.

The time spent getting his family back on solid foods was time spent away from Mia. Even while they were at work, they'd been so swamped—in a good way—they hadn't had many moments to hang out with each other.

Despite the fact that he remained cautious about Mia's impulsiveness, he was missing her something fierce. He missed hearing her laugh at his stupid dad jokes. He missed joining her for lunch and trying her kitchen misadventures. He missed kissing her.

He really missed that.

But more than anything, he missed his friend. And Mia had somehow become not only a woman he was attracted to sexually, but a woman who he looked forward to seeing, talking to, and being around.

When had she become his best friend? How had it happened? He was at a loss. More, the closer they became as friends, the more he wanted her.

He didn't want to compare her to Chrissy, although he felt himself constantly doing so. But he and Chrissy had never been friends. Their relationship started out with lust and passion. Maybe that was another reason why it had eventually ended. When all that exciting passion fizzled, there was nothing left.

With Mia, there was so much more. If he never got to kiss her, hug her, touch her again, he knew he would still want her in his life.

"We have an expert in our midst. Lincoln McMann is here."

The sound of his name and the accompanying applause pulled Linc out of his thoughts. This wasn't the first workshop he'd attended at the conference where the presenter called him out. He didn't mind. Much.

Linc stood and waved, jostling the conference room table as he did so. He might be "an expert" in IT but he was still as clumsy as ever. He grabbed his cup of coffee before the dark liquid sloshed onto the table.

"Anything you'd like to add to the presentation?" the presenter asked.

Since Linc had been daydreaming about Mia throughout most of the presentation, he really had no idea what the presenter had talked about or which direction he had taken the topic. Oops.

"Nope. Nothing from me. You did a great job," he said to another round of applause. The presenter grinned proudly.

Linc had been to several workshops in the two days they'd been at WMSM World. He had gathered some knowledge and a few tips and tricks to try out when he returned to the office. At the same time, he should have accepted their initial offer to be a keynote speaker. He knew he could have done well imparting the wisdom he gained over the last decade.

When the session ended, Linc made his way toward the exhibit hall, where vendors had set up booths to display different products and services. He had promised Mia he would meet her there and then they were going to grab lunch before the afternoon workshops.

Even though the exhibit hall was large, it didn't take him long to find her. He spotted that pretty strawberry blonde hair and her tall stature right away. He walked toward the booth where she was busy talking to an exhibitor.

For her part, Mia was working it. She flitted from booth to booth, gathering information and chatting up the vendors. She'd even gone out to dinner with some of them the night before, a fact that Linc hadn't been too happy about. He'd been hoping they could share a meal together and catch up. She'd invited him to join her, but in the end, he'd spent the night on FaceTime with the kids as he enjoyed a rubbery-tasting chicken from room service.

After she left the third booth, he made his presence known. "Hey, you," he said.

A huge smile blossomed on her face. She rushed toward him, her hands full of brochures, swag, and other marketing materials.

"I have so many ideas. I can't wait to implement—" She cut herself off and took a breath. "I mean, as soon as I return to the office, I'm going to type up everything I've learned and present it to you and Nadine. But I know you'll love all the changes I'm going to propose."

More changes. Linc clamped down on the flash of anxiety her words incited.

"Any word from the kids?"

The fact that she asked about his kids at all made that anxiety dissipate slightly. It was replaced by a warm feeling.

"Are they having fun with grandma and grandpa?" she asked.

His parents had arrived the day before he left for New Jersey. He couldn't tell who had been more excited, the twins or his parents. In any case, his house had been a flurry of happy activity, hugs, kisses, and laughter. The kids showed off their new kittens and, even though he told them not to, his parents had brought presents.

"I called my mom this morning. Everyone is having a great time. Did I tell you that I let the kids stay home from nursery school this week?"

"You did." Mia smiled. "But you can tell me again."

And for that, he was eternally grateful. Most people, even the ones with kids of their own, got sick of hearing him talk about his children. But not Mia.

She put everything in her hands into her cross-shoulder bag. "Ready for lunch?"

"I'm starved," he admitted. "Feel like a burger?"

"Sounds great. Let's head up to that place on the first floor."

They made their way out the expo hall, with Mia only stopping at two more booths.

"How was the workshop?" Mia asked as they walked toward the restaurant. She looked fresh and pretty in a gold dress, high boots and matching headband, kind of mod, like a model from the Sixties.

"Meh."

She wagged a finger at him. "You should have taught one of the workshops. I knew you weren't going to learn anything here."

"I have happened to pick up a few things actually."

She ignored that comment. "Why didn't you accept their offer to speak? I mean, I know you didn't want to leave the kids. But any other reason? Fear of public speaking?"

He smiled. "Nope. Surprisingly. I don't really enjoy being the center of attention, but once I start talking about a subject I know well, I can really get going."

"Then why didn't you agree to speak at the conference?"

He shrugged nonchalantly. Only, Linc knew exactly why he hadn't accepted. From the look on Mia's face, she knew he had an actual reason too.

"I would love to impart my knowledge on websites and anything IT or computer-related," he began. "But whenever I get to the part where I ask for any questions it never fails that I get asked about my former company."

"What's wrong with that?"

Fair question. "I am usually asked about the, um, money side of my last company. How much I made and what I did with it. Do I give to any charities? Somehow those questions tend to lead to more personal questions about my life in general."

"Ah. Not a fan of the personal questions."

"Not really. Some things I can discuss or steer in certain directions. But when they ask about my children or my wife, er, ex-wife…"

He trailed off and Mia didn't pick up the conversation. Instead, she beelined toward a window display set up in one of the many shops that lined the first floor of the hotel.

"Look at this." She pointed to a mannequin wearing a black dress. Mia was practically drooling over the dress that managed to be both sexy and classy at the same time.

"It's nice," he offered.

"It's way more than nice," she said, tapping a finger against her lips.

Linc took a better look at the dress, trying to figure out what was so awe-inspiring about it. It was long and form-fitting. "You know, I don't think I've ever seen you wear black. You always have on lots of colors."

Mia smiled. "That's because when I worked in the bridal shop, I had to wear black all day, every day. When I started working for Something True, I decided I was going to brighten up things."

She'd certainly done that.

She bit her lip as she continued to study the dress. "I did bring something to wear tonight, but this dress. Oh."

Lunch had to wait a little longer as Mia went into the store, tried on the dress, and eventually ended up buying it. Linc's stomach was screaming hungry noises in protest, but he couldn't complain too much when he saw how happy buying one little dress made Mia.

"I can't believe you didn't let me see you in that dress," he said as they sat down at a table for lunch.

Mia blushed. "Well, I kind of want to surprise you tonight at the gala."

"Surprise me?" He already knew she looked great in everything she put on.

She reached across the table and grabbed his hand. "Yeah. You and I, well, we haven't exactly had much time together. Alone, I mean."

She could say that again.

"I miss you," she said softly.

It was possible he stopped breathing. Linc knew they were in a crowded restaurant in the middle of a packed hotel. Yet, the way Mia had her gaze locked on his made him feel like they were the only two people in the world.

He didn't know how to respond, so he tried to keep it light. "We won't exactly be alone tonight in the middle of a big gala."

"True." She squeezed his fingers. "But there's always... after."

Linc gulped. He couldn't deny he'd thought about spending "alone time" with Mia. How could he when he'd specifically packed some essential adult-alone-time items of the foil packet variety, just in case. He couldn't remember the last time he'd even purchased condoms, let alone used them.

"After," he repeated.

Mia nodded, her pretty eyes practically sparkling.

Yes, there was after the gala. And then, there was after that. After this conference was over. After they were back in Alexandria.

Wasn't that what really scared him?

***

198

"I can't believe we won!" Nadine was glowing as she held up the small statue they got for first place.

Mia had really enjoyed the conference. She'd gotten a thrill interacting with other people who were doing the same kind of work, even in different industries. There was so much information to learn and gather.

Tonight had been fun too. There had been a cocktail hour first, followed by dinner. For a mass-produced hotel ballroom meal, it hadn't been too bad. The conference had put some time and money into the décor. The ballroom was large, but somehow with the lighting and staging, it felt intimate and fancy.

Speaking of fancy, she ran a hand down her new black cocktail dress. She didn't know what made her happier, the way the dress fit her like a glove or the way Linc's eyes had practically popped out of his head when she'd met him at the cocktail hour.

The last month had been busy and Mia had felt the absence of Linc acutely. She'd gotten used to talking, laughing, joking with him each day. Of course, she completely understood when the kids had gotten sick. But she had to admit that it had hurt a little when he'd said no to her offer to help.

She had hoped he wasn't pulling back from her. There was a definite possibility that he was still ruffled about her getting the kids kittens. Now that she knew more about Chrissy and their marriage, she got it.

Mia got the impression that Linc was somehow comparing her with his ex-wife. That was unfair because she didn't think she was anything like the woman he described.

Still, she could appreciate that he still had issues to work out. She only wished he would let her help him, instead of putting up a wall.

She'd stayed busy over the last few weeks. She'd checked off several other items from her to-do list, including goat yoga, which was just as it sounded: yoga with goats. And she was still laughing about it. She'd dragged her sister along and once the goats were standing on their backs, both Mia and Emerson had completely lost it.

Mia had also been invited by an old friend from college to take part in a polar bear plunge in the Potomac River. It had sounded pretty easy at first. But it had been two weeks and she still wasn't sure if her toes had thawed.

Most exciting had been finding the perfect company to take her skydiving. She'd done her research and set a date.

Linc hadn't seemed too happy for her though when she told him about it. At least it gave them something to talk about. In a month of sick kids, busy work schedules and the possibility that Linc was avoiding her, Mia would take any opportunity to be with him.

She'd even had a plan coming into this conference. A very unprofessional plan that involved a hotel room, some champagne, and acting on the feelings she could no longer suppress when it came to Linc.

She'd really hoped—crossed all fingers and toes and wished on stars—that the time apart would help diminish her feelings. Instead, what she felt for Linc only grew. She'd had no intention to become involved with someone so soon after the end of her marriage. In fact, she'd actively opposed the very notion. Yet, Mia knew she could no longer deny what was between her and Linc.

He made her feel differently than anyone in her life ever had. When Linc looked at her, it felt like he was really seeing her. More than that, he saw something in her that she was only beginning to see herself.

Mia hadn't intended to become involved with any man for a good long time. Despite what her sister may think, she did value Emerson's opinion, and she got why her sister had dissuaded her from pursuing Linc. They worked together. He was her boss. He was a single father. He had issues to work through from his marriage.

So did she. But in finding out what kind of woman she was, all roads seemed to lead back to Linc.

But she'd been so busy being wined and dined by different people she'd met in Atlantic City that she hadn't been able to enact her plan yet. And tonight was her last chance. Mia knew she needed an edge and the black dress with just a touch of lace accents did the trick.

In fact, she'd felt his eyes on hers all night. He'd even held her hand as they read the nominees from their category.

There were many award categories and Mia had anxiously awaited the Best Up & Coming Website award, which wasn't announced until near the end. When they called out Something True, she couldn't believe it. They had won the whole category.

"We are the winners," Nadine said.

"You keep saying that. It's almost been an hour." Linc shook his head.

They were enjoying their drinks at their table. Waiters were cleaning up the plates and remnants of dinner as the attendees gathered around the many bars in the ballroom, or made their way to the dance floor where a DJ was playing a variety of songs.

She pushed the statue in his face. "But it's so pretty. Look, it's gold with Something True inscribed right here next to first freaking place."

"You're ridiculous."

"And a winner," she added. "Now, I'm going to celebrate by grabbing that cutie by the bar. I have moves to show him on the dance floor.

Mia glanced toward the bar where a super-hot twenty-something was ordering a drink.

"Nadine!" Linc said in an exasperated voice. "He looks like a baby."

"So?"

"So, you are probably old enough to be his—"

"Finish that sentence and I will beat you with this first place statue."

Mia stifled a laugh. To be fair, the hottie at the bar had been making eyes at Nadine for the last twenty minutes.

Nadine reapplied her lipstick and then stood. She made her way in the direction of the bar and Mia had no doubt that the young guy didn't stand a chance.

"Come on," she said to Linc.

"Where?"

"We're dancing too."

"Uh…you do recall what happened the last time we danced? You angling to move in and take care of me again?"

Mia rolled her eyes. Dramatically, so Linc would notice. "We're not salsa dancing. Just slow dancing. You barely have to move. Let's go."

She grabbed his hand and led him to the middle of the dance floor. The music changed and a very romantic song started playing as soon as Linc put his arms around her.

Perfect, she thought.

They began swaying to the music, both staying silent for a few minutes. She was enjoying being held by Linc. He smelled amazing. The cologne he was wearing was subtle, but it had a musky aroma that she found utterly intoxicating. Plus, he looked amazing in his dark suit. He'd kept his glasses on, which just added a whole other layer of sex appeal.

"You know, I probably haven't told you this enough." A wrinkle appeared on his forehead. "Or maybe I haven't told you at all."

Curious, she tilted her head as they continued to sway. "What's that?"

"You're doing really well at your job."

Heat radiated throughout her chest.

"Actually, you're doing really well at your job and as a communications professional. Have you ever thought about going into comms or marketing?"

"I majored in communications in college."

"No kidding.

"I used to do a lot of the communications and marketing, and PR now that I'm thinking about it, for my mom's store. I started all of their social media and was the one maintaining everything. I used to write newsletters and the ad copy. I enjoyed it."

"Maybe we need to hire a new person for your job and move you to a different position."

Her first reaction was to wave off the compliment. But that was what the old Amelia would do. The new and improved Mia grinned. "I think I would love that. But I should remind you that I've only been with the company for a couple months."

"Why waste talent?"

Talent? Linc thought she had talent? Talent that didn't center around the way she walked down a runway or the way she looked?

Mia momentarily forgot about everything else happening around her. Her skin was tingling in the most delightful way as she took a moment to absorb his words.

"Are you okay?" Linc asked.

Never better. To prove it, she went on tiptoe and pressed her lips to his. It had been some time since they'd kissed. She'd meant it to last no more than a second, but as soon as they were mouth to mouth, the kiss deepened. Her arms wound even tighter around his neck. His hands grasped at the back of her black dress.

When they pulled apart, he wore the most adorable lop-sided grin. "Not that I mind, but what was that for?"

"You have no idea what your words meant to me. Thank you."

Then he surprised her by kissing her again. It was a hungry and possessive kiss. It left her feeling light-headed.

"What was that for?" she asked, her eyes still closed as she tried to center herself.

"Because I've wanted to do that all night." His eyes pinched together. "I've wanted to do it this entire conference actually." He shook his head. "I've wanted it to do since the last time, which was almost a month ago."

She grinned. He was so adorable. "Ditto," she said a bit breathlessly.

The DJ was still going strong, but the dance floor was beginning to thin out. Mia glanced around, searching for Nadine. She spotted her just as Nadine and her young hottie rounded the corner. She couldn't stifle the smile.

"What's that about?" Linc asked, tapping the edge of her mouth.

She wasn't sure how he would react to Nadine leaving with a man. "Oh nothing. Just feeling happy tonight."

She wasn't sure if this was the right. Then again, would there ever be a right time?

"Linc, there's something I've always wanted to do and I would love it if you came along."

"You know I support you trying all these new things but there is no way in hell you're getting me to jump out of a plane."

She couldn't help but laugh. "No, not that. Although, I did reserve a time."

He frowned. "You know I'm not on board with you doing that. You couldn't, say, go to a trampoline park instead?"

She laughed again. "No. It's supposed to be the ultimate adrenaline rush. I'm jumping out of a plane and you are going to have to deal."

"What's this other thing then?" he asked. "You want to head to Mars or make your way to the bottom of the ocean and visit the Titanic?"

"Oh, ha ha. Aren't you funny."

He kissed the tip of her nose.

"Actually, I'd kind of like to gamble. You know, play some slots or blackjack or roulette. Something. Anything."

His head fell back in relief. "You've never been to a casino?"

"Not really. I had a couple pageants in hotels that had casinos. But I was obviously too young to play. I've always wanted to."

"Since we're in Atlantic City, I do believe that can be arranged."

Again, she reached for his hand, intertwining their fingers. "Yeah. Let's go."

He laughed. "Are you ready to gamble?"

She glanced down at their joined hands and then back up into his eyes. She saw the touch of lust there. It had to mirror her own.

Was she ready to gamble? More than she could say.

Chapter Thirteen

They didn't stay in the casino too long. But Mia was thrilled they went, and not only because she won a hundred dollars playing roulette.

The lights, the sounds, the energy, all of it was infectious. People were gathered around a craps table, yelling excitedly. A group of women wearing tiaras and sashes were occupying one of the blackjack tables as they talked and giggled. The bells and sparkles from the slot machine area were contagious. Of course, it had taken only five minutes to go through twenty-five dollars at the slots. Mia could totally see how people got addicted to casinos.

The free drinks didn't hurt either.

But there was something else she was becoming addicted to, and that something, er, someone, was standing next to her in the elevator smelling amazing, looking hot and emitting sexual vibes. It couldn't be her imagination, Mia knew it. They were alone in the gold-plated elevator and she could see their reflections in the mirrored doors. If they were a cartoon, there would have been little hearts shooting over their heads.

Neither of them said a word. When the elevator reached their floor, they still didn't speak. Nor did they as they walked down the long hallway toward their rooms, which were only a few doors apart. They reached room 1217 first.

"This is me," Linc said. But he made no move to unlock the door.

"Right," she said. Mia wanted to cringe. She was so not good at this. A seductress, she was not.

"Well," Linc continued, looking a bit nervous. His eyes were darting up and down the empty hallway. "I guess it's late."

"Oh." She couldn't keep the disappointment from her voice.

"I mean, it's not *too* late." He shuffled his feet.

Hope welled up inside her. "No, it's not too late."

"That is, we're both adults. I'm used to the kids' bedtime, that's all. It would be late for them."

"Right. Well, I'm not a kid. Neither are you." This was possibly the dumbest conversation she'd ever had.

Mia had never really been great at flirting. She'd always preferred to just be herself. But Linc was even worse than she was. Realizing that, she quickly decided she'd have to be the one to move the situation along. If she didn't, they could spend the entire night standing in this hallway.

She took a quick breath and blurted out, "Do you want me to come in for a bit? To your room."

His eyes widened. "Sure. Really?" He ran a hand through his hair. "I do want you to come inside. But you're okay with that?"

She noticed that during his rambling he'd managed to remove his hotel keycard from his pocket. She reached for it and pressed it into the slot that unlocked the door. When the green light appeared, she pushed the door open and walked in.

"Yes, I'm definitely okay with it," she said over her shoulder.

Linc had left one of the bedside lights on. Other than that, the room was masked in darkness, save for the light pouring in from the boardwalk and other hotels through the window. It was a replica of her room so she knew where everything was. She put her clutch on the console next to the door and turned back to Linc, who hadn't moved yet.

"Come in," she said. "This is your room after all."

"And you're in it." He had a bit of a dazed expression as he finally, slowly, crossed the threshold and followed her into the room.

Now that she was inside, Mia had no idea what to do. She walked to the window and peered out.

"It's a nice view," Linc said from right behind her.

"Yeah, it's…" The exact same view she had from her room. And who cared anyway. She didn't invite herself into Linc's room to stare at other hotels.

"Oh, god, Linc. What are we doing?" She couldn't take it anymore. This was ridiculous. She wanted him and she would bet anything that he felt the same way.

"I want to be here," she said.

"I'm a little amazed that you are. When you took the key-card from me, I felt like my high school self, that shy nerdy kid who had a crush on you from afar. The last couple minutes felt dreamlike."

"But we both want to be here. Right?" she asked, biting her lip.

"Oh, hell yes."

"And neither of us are in high school any longer," she said.

"Amen to that. We're consenting adults."

There was a long silence that followed his words. Then, simultaneously, they both started laughing.

"Wow, neither of us has any game." Mia started laughing even harder.

"We're both fairly pathetic." Linc was laughing so hard he actually started coughing.

"It's a wonder either of us were able to get married at all," she said, wiping a tear from her eye.

"I expected more out of you," Linc said, holding his side. "You were homecoming queen. You should be used to this kind of thing."

"And yet, I'm as clueless as you. Maybe I should return my tiara."

"But I am happy you're here, Mia. Really happy. Ecstatic actually."

She studied him. Linc was so handsome. He was tall and built. But he had the most adorable face and she loved his lop-sided smile. His hair needed a trim. It was falling into his eyes at the moment. And those eyes, well, they were darker than usual. And aimed directly at her.

It took her breath away.

"I'm ecstatic too. You make me feel…different," she decided.

He cocked his head. "Different?"

"Better," she quickly amended. "You make me feel better than anyone else in my life. Like, you see this version of me that is invisible to everyone else."

He opened his mouth, but she quickly stepped forward to stop him. "You believe in me and I can't tell you how much that means to me."

The laughter from only a minute ago stopped. It was as if something changed in the air. Her breath was suddenly coming fast. Mia put a hand to his chest. If she pressed hard enough maybe it would stop beating so hard.

Linc seemed as dazed as she was. He was watching her with an intensity she rarely saw from him.

"I do believe in you, Mia. I think you're, well…"

"Well what?" she asked, truly curious.

He cupped her cheek, and the gesture was so sweet and comforting she almost wept. No one had ever looked at her like this before. Like she was the only woman in the world and everything she did was amazing.

"I think you are smart and funny and beautiful. I know you're on your own journey right now, but even getting to be a small part of it has been so rewarding."

"Oh, Linc."

"You're more capable than you realize. I can't wait until you discover it all yourself."

Capable. No one had ever said that to her. She couldn't recall any romcoms or romance novels where the word capable made an appearance, and yet, it was the most romantic thing he could have said to her.

She took a few steps back, assessing him as she did. How had she gotten lucky enough to have him in her life again?

"Linc, you are an amazing father." Her cheeks were growing warm. "And you've been the most awesome friend to me."

At the mention of *friend* Linc's smile faltered.

"But I already have a lot of friends. I'm ready for something more. With you."

They rushed to each other. Before she questioned anything they were kissing. Their arms wrapped around each other tightly. Their breath was rushing out in gasps. Their bodies were trying to fuse together as they toppled onto the bed.

Linc covered her body with his and the feel of his weight was heady. She ripped her mouth from his as a satisfied groan escaped.

His hands began moving all over her body, eliciting an almost electric shock everywhere they touched.

She started losing sense of time. They kissed and touched each other for what could have been either thirty seconds or thirty minutes. Mia had no idea. All she was aware of was how good Linc made her feel.

Then, clothing started coming off in a flurry. Mia wasn't even sure who was taking off what. She knew her bra had been unclasped and she started laughing when she saw it flying across the room. She reached for Linc's pants, wanting to pull down the zipper, but they'd already been removed.

"More," she said on a half laugh.

"There's not much left," he said, breathlessly.

To prove him wrong, she reached down and pulled the waistband of his boxer briefs. She let them snap back at his skin.

"Touché," he said to her.

"Off," she responded.

After some wiggling and adjusting they were both naked. Skin to skin. Heartbeat to heartbeat. Linc was perched over her, resting on his elbows as their most intimate areas were lined up and ready to become one.

Mia was overcome with emotions. Happiness and excitement at the forefront. But beyond that, she couldn't help feeling the anxiety of how this moment was going to change everything. She'd wanted to transform this year and now she was, with Linc at her side.

"You're beautiful, Mia," Linc said. "Inside and out." He brushed his lips gently against her mouth. "You're only starting to see it now. But I've been aware since we were young. You are truly extraordinary."

His words made her want to weep, but in the best way possible. She didn't know how to respond, so she kissed him back. Long and with as much passion and feeling as she could muster.

As the lights from Atlantic City filtered in through the window and coated them in a neon glow, they began to move as one. Finally, expressing how much they were both extraordinary.

***

Linc could not believe what had just happened.

Not that he was complaining. Far from it.

He'd wanted to spend more time with Mia. He'd missed being with her. But what occurred between them in this room went far beyond his expectations.

He was propped against the pillows, with Mia curled up next to him. Her hand was tracing lazy patterns on his bare chest, as he took stock of his body. Feeling both exhausted and full of energy at the same time, Linc let out a long exhale.

"You okay?" she asked, looking up at him, her blue eyes clear as the morning sky.

"More than okay," he said and kissed her softly. "You?"

"Never better," she said with a big smile. "Although, I am a little thirsty. Got anything to drink?"

"Yes, in the mini fridge. I have a couple waters. Let me—"

She pushed him back down when he began to get up. Then she flopped on top of him again and kissed him long and hard. His arms immediately went around her and held on tight.

She giggled as he took control and assaulted her mouth. Rolling her under him, he decided to give an encore of their previous performance.

An hour later, they were lazing about in the room. The TV was on in the background. He'd run down to the first floor and bought some snacks for them. Mia was wearing one of his t-shirts, her panties, and nothing else as she watched whatever was currently airing on Bravo. Her beautiful cocktail dress had been hung in his closet.

He excused himself to wash his face. While he was in the bathroom, his mind decided to go crazy with different possibilities and ideas. Did this mean that he and Mia were now in a relationship? Could they make a relationship work between them?

He wasn't sure. Feeling overwhelmed, Linc took a moment to breathe deeply and assess the situation. Had the bathroom been bigger he would have started pacing.

Getting involved with someone had been far from his mind. He'd been focusing solely on the kids for what felt like way longer than the four years they'd been on this Earth.

But things were different now. Mia was around. And he wanted her to be around.

She was good with the kids. More than good, really. She was great, amazing. Hadley and Hugo had both taken to her. She always asked about them before anything else. Never once did she get in the way of his relationship with them.

Yet, guilt was starting to seep in at the mere idea of bringing someone else into their world. He didn't want them to feel that there was anyone more important than they were.

Linc left the bathroom and saw that Mia had changed the channel and was now watching some home improvement show.

"I can't wait to have a house again. I loved decorating my last one," she said, without turning around.

That was another issue. Was Mia truly ready to be in another serious relationship? Her marriage hadn't ended all that long ago. How would she feel about the twins being in her life? Because anyone who dated Linc would have to be okay with his children.

"Oh," she said suddenly, swiveling around to face him. "I saw the cutest stuffed animal down in the gift shop for Hugo. I think he would love it."

Linc tried to speak, but no words came out.

"I haven't seen anything for Hadley yet though. But we need to find her the perfect present."

He was beyond touched. That's what he wanted to tell her. He needed her to know that her caring about his children, of even thinking about gifts for them, meant the world to him.

This could work. Him and Mia. The kids and Mia. Him and the kids and Mia. His job with Mia working there too.

From across the room, he could hear his cell ringing. It was near Mia.

"Mia, who's calling? Spam?"

"No, it's, oh. It's your mom."

The hairs on the back of his neck stood up. He'd told his parents to call once a day to give a report on the kids. They'd refused, as he knew they would. Every time he'd texted either his mom or dad asking for an update, they told him to stop worrying. They said everything was fine and everyone was having a blast.

The fact that his mom was calling now—especially at this hour—wasn't good. The kids should have been long in bed by now.

He rushed toward Mia, who had his phone. She quickly handed it over.

"What's wrong?" he answered, without so much as a hello.

"It's not that bad," his mom said in way of a greeting.

"What happened?" He heard a muffled noise in the background. Kind of like a microphone or announcement. "Where are you?"

"In the hospital."

His heart dropped. "The hospital?"

Mia gasped. "Oh my god, what happened?" She came to stand right in front of him.

"Shh," he said irritably.

"It's Hugo. He broke his arm."

216

Shit. A million thoughts ran through his head. Did he leave an insurance card for his parents? Which hospital were they at? Did he know any doctors there? Would Hugo need surgery?

The most prevalent thought was his undoing. *I should be there.*

"Is he okay? Where's Hadley?"

"What's going on?" Mia asked impatiently.

"Hugo is in the hospital. He broke his arm," he whispered in a rushed tone.

His mom continued. "Hadley is at home with your father."

Linc gripped the phone harder. His palm was sweating. "How did it happen?"

"Hugo takes after you, Linc. He's a big klutz, too. All he was doing was walking backward. He just fell over, but when he landed, he had braced his fall on his left arm. It broke in two places. Unlike his dad, he's being a trooper. Aren't you, Hugo?"

"He's there?" Linc said, feeling a slight relief already. He had been imagining his son alone on a gurney somewhere.

"Right next to me. Hold on, I'll put him on the phone."

Linc talked to his son, but it did nothing to calm his nerves. Hugo had to be in a ton of pain, but he was putting on a brave front. "I'm proud of you for being so strong, Hugo."

"Can we watch Star Wars when you get back from your trip?"

Linc laughed, half out of nervous energy. "Of course. We can watch anything you want."

"Cool. Can I talk to Ms. Mia?"

"Uh…" Linc was shocked.

Slowly, he handed the phone to Mia. "He asked to speak to you."

Mia took the phone. While she talked to Hugo, Linc was assaulted by a myriad of emotions. Anger, fear, concern, relief. But watching Mia talk and laugh with his son left him at a loss. He had no idea how to feel about the way she cooed to him or the fact that Hugo had asked for her at all.

Finally, Mia handed the phone back. "It's your mom again," she said.

His mom sighed. Linc wondered how long she'd been at the hospital.

"They x-rayed and determined the bone cracked in two locations. Hugo will need a cast for about six weeks. Unfortunately, the arm is too swollen tonight, so he'll need to come back tomorrow for them to apply the cast. I'll bring him here around—"

"I'll bring him," Linc said in a stern voice, interrupting his mother. He was supposed to stay in Atlantic City until tomorrow night. He'd told everyone it made more sense to wait out the traffic, when in reality, he'd wanted to spend more time with Mia alone.

"No, Linc, the worst is over. Enjoy—"

Again, he had to interrupt. "Don't even try to tell me to enjoy my trip. You know I'm only going to think about Hugo until I see him again. I'll be there tomorrow," he said definitely.

After he disconnected the call, he did the only thing he could think to do. He turned on Mia.

"I should have been there. It should be me at the hospital. I'm his father."

"I'm sorry, Linc." She came toward him, but he backed up. "I can't imagine how worried you are."

"No, you can't. And maybe if I had been home instead of here in Atlantic City at a conference that you found, this accident would have never happened."

"Like you just said, it was an accident…wait a minute." First, confusion clouded her eyes. But it was quickly replaced with something else. Something much more potent. Hurt.

"Linc," she said warily.

He shook his head. "Don't." He didn't want to hear anything she had to say. He didn't want to hear anything from anyone. All he wanted was to be with his son, to hold him and comfort him. Instead, he was stuck three states away from him.

"I never wanted to come to this conference. Why couldn't you have left well enough alone?"

"Well enough…" She trailed off. A little line formed on her forehead as her eyes pinched together. "This was all for work, Linc."

"Why did you have to enter that contest? If you hadn't, I would have been home when my child was injured. Hell, he probably wouldn't have been injured at all."

She glanced down at her bare feet. It dawned on Linc that she was wearing very little clothing. The same could be said for him.

Because they'd just slept together.

And just like that, his world came crashing down around him. This is why getting involved with a woman would never work. He'd allowed Mia to infiltrate his very well-constructed walls the same way he'd let his ex-wife in.

Her lip quivered, but he ignored it.

"Are you blaming me for Hugo's injury?" she asked.

Linc didn't care if he hurt her feelings. The only thing he cared about was his son, who'd gotten hurt because he hadn't been there for him. The reason he'd been away was standing in front of him, wringing her hands together and asking if he blamed her.

He said the only thing he could. "Yes."

***

Pain, pure and simple, slashed through her at Linc's reply.

He couldn't be serious. Could he? He was holding her responsible for what happened to Hugo hundreds of miles away?

Before her temper rose, Mia checked herself. Linc had just found out his son's arm was broken. She couldn't imagine what he was going through. Linc probably felt so helpless. She definitely had to give him an out. She pushed the hurt down that his words had evoked and decided to do something productive again.

She rushed to the bathroom and snatched up all of Linc's toiletries. Luckily, his bathroom wasn't the disaster that hers was. She shoved everything in his dopp kit. Then she returned to the main room where Linc remained standing, still as stone.

"What are you doing?" he finally asked.

"Gathering your things." She found his bag in the closet, flung it onto the bed and unzipped it. "So we can take off and go home."

"We?"

"Well, yeah. We need to get to Hugo."

220

"I need to get to Hugo. My son. Not yours."

She froze. As true as they may be, those two little words were like a knife going into her chest. *Not yours.*

She stepped backward from the bed and put a hand to her cheek as if she'd been slapped. She knew her reaction was ridiculous. Of course, Hugo wasn't hers. Neither was Hadley.

Maybe Linc wasn't either.

After tonight…well, they'd been intimate. Finally. The evening had been amazing and wonderful. At least, it had been for her.

But the way Linc was looking at her—staring daggers really—only made her already-over-active heartbeat speed up even more. She felt horrible even thinking it, but she wasn't only worried about Hugo. She was concerned for herself too. Something had shifted and whatever connection they'd had between them had been broken.

"Linc," she said softly. "You can't seriously blame me for what went down tonight."

He worked his jaw, moving it back and forth. "You have brought nothing but chaos into my life."

Suddenly cold, she rubbed her arms. "Excuse me?"

"Do you have any idea how hard I've worked to establish order and stability for my children?"

He didn't get it. Even as he said the words, she could tell he was clueless. It wasn't only Hadley and Hugo who needed a calm environment. "Also, for yourself."

His eyes flashed an emotion she didn't quite comprehend. "Yes, for myself as well." He threw a hand into the air. "So what? After what I've been through, I deserve a little peace."

"Yes, you do. But you're living too safely, Linc. Any little ripple comes along, and you freak out as if a tidal wave was heading in your direction."

"You have been that tidal wave. First, the dance lessons."

"That was your idea." No way was she going to stand here and just take his attack. "And besides, you said you didn't blame me for your ankle. Are you just taking that back?"

He ignored her. He plowed right through her breaking heart. "Then the cats."

"Oh my god. Not the cats again. Come on, Linc."

"All I wanted to do was work and go home and be with my kids. But you came along and started changing things at work."

"For the better. You needed more social media. You needed help at the office. You and Nadine can't handle it all. Besides, this contest win is going to be huge."

"We were fine before. I was fine before—"

"Before I came back into your life? Is that what you mean?" She held her breath anticipating his answer. But she didn't have to wait long.

"Yes."

She nodded. What else was there to do? She could still see the rumpled sheets and scattered pillows, fresh from their love-making. It hadn't been that long since they'd held each other and loved each other. Mia didn't jump into bed with just anyone. Tonight meant something to her. Something monumental and important. She'd assumed he'd felt the same way.

He ran a hand through hair that was already mussed. "I can't do this right now, Mia. I have to get back to Hugo. Immediately."

She pointed toward the door. "I'll just grab my stuff." Linc had driven them both up to New Jersey from Virginia.

"No."

"What?"

"I need to go now," he said through clenched teeth.

"I'll only be a couple minutes." She started toward the door, but his words stopped her.

"Look, I know I drove us, but I just can't be in a car with you."

Tears stung her eyes, but she sucked in a sharp breath to keep them at bay.

He grabbed his wallet off the dresser and handed her a wad of folded bills. His arm froze in mid-air and Mia could do nothing but stare at it.

"I know I drove you here. Take this so you can take the bus or train home." He pulled out more bills. "Or rent a car."

It reminded her so much of Charlie. Her ex never took the time to really see her. Or hear her. Or even attempt to feel what she was going through.

How many times had she tried to tell Charlie she was unhappy or discontent? She'd attempted to share her feelings, but he'd brushed her aside every time.

Why don't you go shopping today?

Just spend some time at the spa. You'll feel better.

As long as you get yourself together for my client dinner tonight….

He'd given her presents that he'd put zero thought into. One time, he'd countered her attempt at sharing her heart with a gorgeous sapphire necklace. The problem was that he'd already given her that exact same necklace for her previous birthday. She'd exchanged the necklace for other jewelry, and he hadn't noticed that either.

His assistant Meryl had slipped up a couple times too. Mia's name would be spelled wrong on bouquets of flowers. Packing slips would be left in presents with Meryl's contact information.

They'd been on one of his business trips in Arizona when Mia finally worked up the nerve to talk to him. She was going to tell him in no uncertain terms that she was very unhappy and considering leaving him. Once again, he didn't have time to hear it. Instead, he'd flung his credit card at her and told her to go nuts.

Like shopping would fix their marriage problems.

More, the gesture had belittled her. Things not working out, throw some money at it.

It's exactly what Linc was doing now.

Never in a million years had Mia thought she would be comparing Linc and her ex-husband. Yet, here they were.

Her stomach contracted. Maybe from the effort of holding back tears. She bit down on her lip and straightened her shoulders. She would not let him see her cry. Nor would she accept money from him.

With one last glance at the cash in his hand, she steeled herself to meet his gaze. She saw anger and she understood that. He was frustrated by being separated from his kids. But that was no excuse for being mean. For dismissing her. She cared about Hugo too and wanted to share in Linc's worry.

But it was clear that Linc didn't want that.

Mia had been desperately trying to better herself the last couple of months. She wanted to be the star of her own life. She needed to prove to herself that she could be independent and strong. She may not be one hundred percent there yet, but her self-confidence had grown by leaps and bounds. There was no way she would allow Lincoln McMann, or anyone for that matter, to treat her this way.

With one last glare, she turned from him and his outstretched hand of money and walked out the door. As the heavy wood clicked into place behind her, she walked down the hallway to her room, never looking back.

She would never look back again.

Chapter Fourteen

Mia returned to her townhouse toting a heavy suitcase and even heavier emotional baggage.

The day turned out to be cloudy and gray. A perfect complement to her mood. The entire trip home had been surreal, with Mia feeling completely numb.

After Mia texted her very early in the morning, Nadine had been able to drive her back to Virginia. Of course, her boss had asked about Linc. Mia told her about Hugo's broken arm and how Linc had left in the middle of the night wanting to return to his kids as soon as possible. She thought it was a perfectly legitimate excuse. However, Nadine seemed suspicious.

"Linc loves those kids more than anything in the world, and I can see him wanting to get to Hugo as fast as possible."

Sitting in the front seat of Nadine's black SUV, she'd clasped her fingers together tightly.

"But it seems odd to me that he would abandon you."

"Abandon is a strong word," Mia had said.

"Hm." Nadine had continued to stare straight ahead. "Just seems out of character for him. He didn't even call me."

Mia had let it go. She'd desperately wanted to talk about the situation, but she couldn't reveal everything to Nadine. Her boss. Linc's partner.

Sunday traffic mixed with construction on Interstate ninety-five had added two whole hours to their trip. When they finally reached her townhouse, Mia tried to breathe a sigh of relief, only no relief came. She let herself in the front door and climbed the stairs to the living room, where she found her sister and Grace chatting on the couch. The two women were relaxed, sharing a large bowl of popcorn and laughing at something on TV. Mia was instantly jealous. She sighed loudly, alerting them to her presence.

"Mia," Grace said with a note of surprise in her voice. "I wasn't expecting you for another couple of hours. Weren't you and Linc going to stay today to do some sightseeing?"

Mia threw her suitcase down. Hard. "Change of plans."

She couldn't miss Grace and Emerson exchanging a look. The two of them had known each other for years, and as far as Mia was concerned, Grace was an honorary Dewitt sister. Still, whatever psychic conversation Em and Grace had just communicated had Grace getting up from the couch.

"Good to have you back, Mia. I need to go do some laundry." She squeezed Mia's arm as she passed by.

"Subtle," Mia said to Emerson after Grace left the room.

"Caring," Emerson responded, narrowing her eyes at Mia. "Grace is a good friend to you, and she is clearly giving the two of us a little time and space to talk."

"I don't want to talk." Irritation laced her voice. Despite her statement, Mia flopped onto the couch.

"What happened?" Emerson asked.

"Nothing." She shrugged. "It just wasn't a great conference."

Liar.

Emerson gave her a look that clearly said she wasn't buying it. "You were so excited to go. Come on, what really happened?"

She told her sister about everything. How wonderful the conference actually was, and about winning the award. She even revealed how she and Linc had taken that next step in their relationship.

"Mia, that's amazing," Emerson said, her blue eyes twinkling.

"Yeah, well, it was. But…" she let her words drag into the silence of the living room because she honestly didn't know what to say.

"But what?" Emerson asked, shifting so they were facing each other. "It wasn't good?" she asked, scrunching up her nose.

Despite everything, Mia laughed. "No, the sex was good. Great. Really great." Wouldn't it be easier if the sex had been horrendous? Or if Linc was hideous. Even though he hadn't been kind to her in the end, she knew that wasn't his true nature.

"So what went down?" Emerson urged, touching her arm.

Feeling exhausted, utterly and completely depleted, she recounted the call about Hugo. She still couldn't get Linc's face out of her mind. How scared and panicked he'd looked while he'd listened helplessly on the phone.

"Ah, poor kid. That must have been awful for him," Emerson said.

"Poor Linc," Mia added. "He was…beside himself."

"That's understandable."

"We fought," she told Emerson.

"About what?"

She blew out a long, shaky breath. "He was upset obviously. He…well, he kinda blamed me for taking him away from his kids. He said that I was bringing chaos into his life, both at work and at home. It was my fault that he hadn't been there for Hugo."

"That's ridiculous," Emerson said quickly, her words laced with loyalty for her sister.

"I know it is. Yet—"

"No." Emerson shook her head. "I'm sure Linc was just worried about his son. There is no way he can place blame on you for something that happened hundreds of miles away. You know that, right?"

Mia offered a half nod. There was no confidence behind it.

"Right?" Emerson said, shaking Mia's arm.

She wanted to agree, but somewhere in the back of her mind, she had to wonder. Maybe Linc and his family had been better off before she waltzed into their lives. Maybe she would be better back on her own.

Mia couldn't stop thinking about her ex-husband. Not about Charlie as a person, but the way he treated her. How many times he'd ignored her or dismissed her. When she ended that relationship, she'd promised herself that she would never allow that to happen again. She was going to find her independence and catch up on lost time.

This year had started off as an adventure. She needed to return to that mindset.

"Listen, Em, I think that sleeping with Linc was a mistake."

Emerson leaned forward. Mia waited for her reply, but her sister remained silent. Mia took a deep breath and kept going.

"I have so many things that I want to do. I've missed out on countless adventures and experiences. I really need to forget about Linc and get back to bettering myself."

Emerson nodded very slowly. "Do you?"

Surprised by Emerson's question, Mia took her time answering. "Well, yeah. Don't you think I should get the chance to do all the things that other people did?"

"Do you even want to be doing all of these so-called adventures?"

Yes. Maybe. I don't know.

"Because I have to tell you," Emerson continued, "that I did have what you call the typical college and young twenty-something experience. And I didn't do half the stuff on your list. To be honest, I never really wanted to do most of it."

Feeling defiant, Mia jutted out her chin. She wanted to do some of it. The dance class had been really fun, until Linc hurt his ankle. She loved going to happy hours.

"Do you really want to jump out of a plane?" Emerson asked.

No. Maybe. I don't know.

Mia flung her head into her hands. *Oh God.*

230

"You kept saying the point of having all of those *adventures* was to do the things you missed out on. But I think you made a miscalculation."

Curious, she looked up at her sister. "What's that?"

"New experiences are great. You can have a lot of fun. But the best part is actually learning about yourself. Sometimes what you learn is totally out of left field."

"I'm tired, Em. Can you sum it up for me because I'm not following."

"I have known you for your entire life. But I don't think you're adventure-girl. I think you are family-girl. I think what you really want, what you've always wanted, was a family of your own. Husband, kids, dog or cat, nice home. Family. People who respect you and value you."

As the words came out of Emerson's mouth, Mia closed her eyes. She knew that nothing could be truer. That is what she wanted.

"Over the last couple months, the happiest I've seen you weren't the times you were partying or going to the movies by yourself."

"No?"

Emerson shook her head. "You seemed the most content when you were with Linc and his kids."

"But that's not my life right now."

"But it could be." Emerson ran a hand through her curls. "The reason you're so upset right now is because you're afraid you just lost the thing that you wanted more than anything."

"We fought. Bad."

And Mia felt so damn guilty. Not to mention, she was worried. She loved Hugo so much, and she hoped the little boy was okay and not in too much pain.

"It's not your fault that Hugo broke his arm," Emerson said, as if reading her mind.

"You're right. Of course, you're right about that. But it is my fault that Linc was away from him when he fell."

Again, Emerson shook her head. "No, Mia. It's Linc's fault that he was away from his kids. It was his decision to agree to go with you. In any case, Hugo could have still broken that arm even if Linc was in town. Accidents happen."

Maybe her sister was right. It didn't really matter though. Nothing was going to take away the lump in her throat or the words Linc had said to her the night before.

Mia fell back against the couch cushions. "Thank God Nadine decided to close the office tomorrow. At least, I have another full day before I have to face Linc."

"The hazards of hooking up with your coworker."

"My boss," Mia clarified.

"Oh, Mia. This is a mess."

Absentmindedly, her fingers found the silver A necklace she always wore. She began playing with it, moving the pendant back and forth. "And the fact that there's only three of us in the office is going to make it so much worse. At least if I worked at some huge company, we could avoid each other."

"Again, I'm going to pull the older sibling card on you. I'm older and wiser."

Mia arched an eyebrow, but Emerson ignored it.

"Avoiding this situation isn't going to make it any better. Give it a day for Linc to see his son and calm down. But don't let it fester. Address this head-on."

Mia nodded, even as she knew she wouldn't take her sister's advice.

As it turned out, Mia didn't need to worry. She'd tossed and turned the entire night before returning to work. But in the end, Linc hadn't shown up. He'd called Nadine and said he would be taking a day or two of sick leave to deal with Hugo.

Nadine reassured her that Hugo would be just fine. Linc was overreacting.

By Thursday, Linc was working again, only remotely. He didn't come into the office. Mia wondered if this would be the new norm.

She felt awful. This was his company. Maybe she should start searching for a new job.

On Thursday afternoon, she pulled up a couple job sites during one of her breaks. Luckily, her resume was updated. She'd already added her duties at Something True.

Unfortunately, she hadn't been very careful about her internet query. When she returned from the ladies' room, Nadine was standing in her cubicle. She was holding an invoice, but her eyes were scanning Mia's computer screen.

Mia rushed forward. "Oh, Nadine, I'm not…." She bit her lip. She didn't want to lie to Nadine. She'd become so fond of her. "I mean…I meant to say, ugh."

But Nadine simply offered a curt nod. "I'll take care of this."

Mia had no idea what that meant. If she thought she felt bad before, it was nothing compared to how she felt now.

***

The doorbell rang aggressively on Thursday night. That was the only way to describe the incessant sound. He'd had a headache for almost an entire week straight now and the doorbell definitely didn't help. Linc ran to the front door before one of the kids woke up.

He flung the door open to find Nadine standing there, a sour look on her face.

Before he could get anything out, she said, "I think three days is quite enough hiding."

Then she pushed her way into the house, hitting him in the stomach with her extremely large purse. Did he say purse? Suitcase would be more appropriate.

"Ugh. What do you keep in here?" Hard cover books, bricks, a weight bench?

She answered by removing the black and gray wool cape she wore. She tossed that over his shoulder as well.

"I'm not your man servant, you know," Linc said, hanging the cape up and placing the eight-hundred-pound purse on a bench near the front door.

"I wouldn't know what you are considering I haven't seen you since last week when we were in New Jersey."

He followed her into the kitchen, where she helped herself to a glass of red wine from a bottle Linc had on the counter. She gestured to her glass and then Linc. He shook his head. He wasn't in a good headspace for alcohol.

"In case I forgot to mention it, I had a situation with one of the kids."

Nadine took a sip of her wine, put the glass on the island, and then offered a sympathetic and caring look. "How is Hugo?"

Linc relaxed somewhat. "He's fine. The doctor said his arm will heal up nicely and he'll be as good as new in about six weeks. For now, he's enjoying the attention and new-found fame that a cast brings to a four-year-old in nursery school."

Nadine smiled. "I bet. Speaking of, I'm having something delivered here tomorrow for him. I included a toy for Hadley as well."

"You didn't have to do—"

"Let's get down to business now," Nadine said, interrupting him.

"Is something wrong with the site?" It hadn't even dawned on him that Nadine's visit had to do with Something True.

"No. Everything's fine, except for the fact that my partner has stopped coming to work." She added a pointed glare in his direction.

Linc sighed loudly and rolled his eyes. He gave in and grabbed a beer from the fridge. Hugo's cat Chase snaked in and out between his legs. "What's the problem? I've worked from home before. I wanted to be here in case Hugo needed me."

"Don't lie to me. I've known you for your entire life and you have never lied to me. Not once."

"I'm not—"

"Don't." Nadine interrupted him once again. "Hugo is fine. He's back in school. You just said so yourself."

"Look," Linc began, allowing the frustration and irritation to infiltrate his voice. Nadine raised a brow, but he didn't let that deter him. "We had an agreement when we first started

Something True. You were going to be the public face and I would be the silent, techy-geek partner."

Nadine appeared nonplussed and drank her wine.

"Did you hear me?" he asked. "Silent. As in, do stuff behind the scenes. There is absolutely no reason why I need to be in the office every day when I can do my job from the comfort of my own home."

"And become even more of a hermit than you already are," she said quickly with just the right amount of sass.

"What did you just say?"

Nadine smacked her lips. "Then why didn't you work from home in the past? If telecommuting is an option, and one you apparently prefer, why have you never taken advantage of it before this week?"

"I…" Linc cracked his neck. She had him there. Of course, he'd taken the occasional work from home day, but for the most part he went into their office.

Clearly done with pleasantries, Nadine fixed her gaze on his. "Let's talk about the real issue here."

Frustrated, Linc ran a hand through his hair. "If you're so wise, why don't you just tell me what the real issue is."

Nadine arched an eyebrow again. Damn, she was so good at that. One little twitch of her brow and a gauntlet was thrown down: *You know what the real issue is.*

Linc fell back into a chair, bringing his beer with him, and gripping it tightly the way Hugo still held onto his security blanket.

Belle jumped up onto the island. Linc was supposed to be firm on telling the cat no and getting her down from the kitchen furniture, but he didn't have it in him at the moment. Instead, he scratched behind her ear, causing Belle to let out long and loud purrs.

"The issue is Mia," Linc said quietly.

Saying her name out loud hurt. A lot.

He'd been a total and complete mess this entire week. Hugo's accident was only a tiny part of it. Nadine was right. Hugo was fine. Linc had made it back to Alexandria in record time last weekend. Of course, driving in the middle of the night helped with that. His little boy had been teary-eyed when he'd gotten home. But once they took him back to the hospital and the cast was applied, he'd been good as new. In fact, Linc had wanted him to stay home from nursery school, but Hugo had insisted he go in to show his class his new cast.

Nadine's next statement shocked him. "Mia is only part of the problem."

He wouldn't have been away from home if it hadn't been for Mia. She came in and did her thing at work and the next thing he knew they were crossing state lines. He'd been adamant about not wanting to leave his children. It had been less than two years since the divorce and custody fight.

Neither of which Hadley and Hugo even remembered.

Not to mention that two years was quite a bit of time.

He shook his head. Linc had to stay true to his convictions. He shouldn't have been away from his family.

Nadine covered his hand with her own. "It looks like a million thoughts are running through your head right now."

He nodded. "It's been a lot to think about."

"Yes, it has." Finally, Nadine acquiesced. Her face softened. "Like I said, Mia is part of the problem, but not the whole thing. You've never really dealt with your ex. Or, more to the point, how your ex messed you up."

Mia had said something similar when she'd stayed with him.

"This has nothing to do with her."

"It certainly does." Nadine pulled up a chair next to him. "You're in love with Mia. That's another part of the problem."

Rather than affirming or denying, he said the thing that had been on the tip of his tongue. The thing that he really didn't want to say. "She's wrong for me."

Linc knew it didn't matter if he loved Mia or not. She wasn't right for him. She didn't fit into his world. Instead, she brought chaos and upheaval. That was the exact opposite of what he wanted.

"Let me ask you a question," Nadine said. "In all your time with Chrissy, did you ever feel the way about her that you feel for Mia?"

He grabbed his beer but put it back on the island and shoved it away without drinking it. "What does that have to do with anything?" Linc grumbled. "Chrissy and Mia are so similar."

Nadine let out a mirthless laugh and nailed him with a you've-got-to-be-kidding-me look.

"What?" Linc asked. "They are."

"Tell me how the two of them are the same." She crossed her arms over her chest and waited.

"They're both impulsive and spontaneous."

"Sometimes I think you spend so much time bent over your computers and electronic gadgets that you really miss out on what goes on with the real people. The two of them are nothing alike."

He wanted to protest but Nadine kept going.

Chrissy was impulsive. She was a free-spirit who liked to travel and experience new things. Nothing wrong with that. Until you throw a husband and two young children into the mix."

"Mia is all about new experiences."

"She is right now. But that's not the norm for her. Being footloose and fancy free was in Chrissy's DNA. It's different for Mia. This is a phase. She just got out of a marriage. Who can blame her for wanting to have a little fun."

"A phase?"

"Yes."

"You can't know that."

"Neither can you," Nadine countered. "Have you asked her what she wants long-term? Because my guess is that child does not want to spend her life hopping from one adventure to another."

Sitting back in his chair, Linc thought about it. He guessed he really hadn't discussed the future with Mia. He knew the things she wanted to do in the short term, like cooking classes and going skydiving.

There was also part of him that reverted to his adolescent self when he was around her. He had known in his core that he couldn't date Mia in high school. Maybe she would always be that untouchable woman of his dreams.

Damn, he needed to get a shrink stat.

Next to him, Nadine shifted. With a silent laugh, he realized he already had one.

"What Chrissy put you through was inexcusable," she said. "But that's in the past now. You have the kids. You have a great job. You're financially stable. It's time to let all that pain go and enjoy what's right in front of you."

"Could I really get to be happy?"

"Oh, honey." Nadine wrapped her arms around him and squeezed tightly. Linc hadn't even realized he'd said that line out loud until she did.

But it was true. He'd been happy once. Happier than the rest of his life. But Chrissy had pulled the rug out from under him. Not just once, but twice.

"I want to be with Mia," he whispered into Nadine's neck as she continued to hug him.

She pulled back and smiled. "I know you do. And she wants to be with you. But holing up in this house and avoiding her isn't going to get you the girl."

He stood. "I want to talk to her." As quickly as he rose, he lowered himself back into seat.

"What's the matter?"

"We, uh, fought. In Atlantic City."

Nadine shrugged. "Why people are afraid of fighting is beyond me. Sometimes words need to be exchanged. Feelings need to be shared."

"It was more than that. I, kinda, uh, blamed her for Hugo breaking his arm."

Nadine blinked. "Lincoln McMann, tell me you're joking."

He shook his head slowly. "I wish I could."

"Well, that explains why she's been moping around the office all week looking like she's about to burst into tears at any moment."

"She's been sad?" His chest tightened.

"Now I know why."

Without warning, Nadine whacked him across the back of the head.

"Ow."

"You deserve that. Oh, Linc, how could you blame her for something she had nothing to do with. She probably feels awful."

Linc rubbed his head. "Now I feel awful. Physically."

"Suck it up. We have more important things to discuss."

"Like what?"

"Like how you're going to win Mia back."

"Do you think I have a shot?" he asked.

"Stranger things have happened."

"Gee thanks."

"Always here for you."

And he knew she was. Now, he had to show Mia that he would always be there for her. No matter what.

Chapter Fifteen

She almost chickened out. Almost.

But in the end, Mia knew she would regret backing out of something she'd wanted to do since...forever. Even if it was scary.

However, that ascent into the air didn't make it easy on her. Sitting in the plane, Mia felt like they climbed into the air for hours. Higher and higher as her heart beat faster and faster.

Once they reached an altitude of thirteen thousand feet, everything seemed to speed up. She was strapped against Wells, her tandem flying instructor, as the other passengers launched themselves out of the plane. Mia would be jumping last.

Wells said something but she couldn't quite hear over the sound of the plane and the fear in her gut.

"What?" she yelled.

"Are you ready?" he asked again.

No!

242

Why was she doing this? What was wrong with her? Humans weren't supposed to be flying through the air.

Wells began moving, forcing her to do an awkward crab-type-walk toward the opening in the plane.

Mia thought about her sister and new brother-in-law. Emerson and Jack were waiting for her on the ground, along with Grace and Xander. She wasn't planning on telling her parents about today's activity until her feet were firmly on the ground.

If they ever landed, that is.

She tried to take deep breaths, but she couldn't. Fear paralyzed her. She was about to tell Wells that she'd changed her mind, when he spoke in her ear.

"Here we go."

And then they went. She was outside of the plane, freefalling in the air. All the fear and anxiety and doubt left her mind.

"Keep your eyes open," Wells said into her ear.

How could she not? She was flying! Adrenaline began to flow through her system as she floated with the clouds, her arms outstretched and a huge smile on her face. Then, suddenly, she was jerked backwards. The parachute. She'd completely forgotten about it. Thank god there was an instructor strapped to her back or she probably would have just soared to a very unpleasant ending.

As she began gliding through the air, seeing the earth below, she almost shed a tear. She did it. She jumped out of a plane. She was currently flying through the sky. This was something that she'd always wanted to do.

Before she could even blink, it was almost over. The ground was incredibly close. Wells instructed her to put her legs straight out in front of them. He did the hard work of landing and next thing she knew, she was touching solid ground again.

As she stood on the ground and Wells was unhooking them, Mia just looked around at the open field. That was it. Adrenaline rush ended.

She thought about everything she'd been through in the last couple of years. She remembered her marriage and how optimistic she'd been when she'd first gotten engaged. Likewise, how devastated she'd been to realize she wasn't in a good marriage.

Then there was Linc and the kids. The word devastated didn't begin to describe how she felt over the end of that relationship. She'd loved Linc more than anyone in her life. She still did. She missed him and the kids.

But today was supposed to be about her. She accomplished something she'd wanted to do for years.

When her adrenaline finally subsided, Mia waited for another feeling to take its place. Completeness. Contentment. Something.

Anything.

Instead, she was left standing in the field with nothing.

She'd considered skydiving to be the epitome of danger and excitement. Something she'd secretly wanted to do her entire life. And she did it. So why wasn't she feeling the way she thought she would. She got what she wanted.

Confused, she began walking back to the building that held the skydiving headquarters with Wells at her side. He was going on about how well she did. But Mia could only muster a half smile.

Why wasn't she feeling elated? She reached for her A necklace and began moving it back and forth on her neck as she considered.

Nodding as Wells told her about how to get the video she'd purchased, Mia couldn't shake the feeling that this was wrong. Not the jumping out of a plane. She was glad she'd done it. But something else was off.

Her family and friends deserved to see more from her than whatever weird mood this was, she decided. As she'd done many other times in her life, she plastered a big smile on her face and forced herself to show some enthusiasm.

They reached the side door to the building, but before she went inside, Mia stopped.

"Everything okay?" Wells asked.

"Sure. It's just, I'm wondering where my sister and friends are. I thought they watched from this side of the building."

Wells' face broke into a big grin.

"What?"

He remained silent but nodded toward the front entrance. With a curious feeling, Mia walked around the side of the of the building. When she turned the corner, she expected to see Em, Grace, and their significant others.

But that wasn't the only thing she saw.

Right there in front of the skydiving building, was a whole party of people. As soon as they saw her, applause and cheers erupted. Grace was holding her phone up, clearly recording everything. Mia didn't know where to look first. She spotted balloons and flowers as her sister ran and launched herself at her.

"Mia, congratulations!" Emerson engulfed her in a long and tight hug. "I'm proud of you." Then she shook Mia three times. Hard. "Please, don't ever do that to me again."

Mia laughed. "Don't worry. That's out of my system."

Emerson stepped aside and Mia anticipated hugging Jack next. But she almost passed out when her mother inched toward her.

"Uh…"

"'Uh' is right," Beatrice Dewitt said.

After Mia picked her fallen mouth off the floor, she turned on Emerson. "I can't believe you told Mama."

"I can't believe you jumped out of a plane. You could have hurt yourself. You could have died."

"But she didn't." Mia's father scooped her up in a big hug. "Congratulations, pumpkin."

"Thanks, Daddy."

She couldn't resist sticking her tongue out at her sister.

"That's what you get for scaring me," Emerson said. There was not an ounce of regret for ratting her out on Emerson's face.

Beatrice leaned forward and whispered in Mia's ear. "I've secretly always wanted to skydive myself."

"Mama!" Mia shook her head in disbelief.

"Come on," Beatrice said, grabbing her husband's hand. "Let's go grab some brochures from inside."

"Holy cow. I can't believe—"

Speaking of disbelief. Mia's words trailed off when she focused in on the other people waiting in the small crowd. Grace and Xander were there. So was Nadine, who had mentioned the possibility of coming out to see her jump.

But right there front and center were three people she would have never expected to be standing there. Three people she desperately wanted to see.

Linc, Hadley and Hugo.

The kids were holding a big sign that read *congratulations* and it was clear they had added their own artwork to it. Linc was holding flowers. When she looked in their direction, the twins started jumping up and down.

Finally, that feeling she'd been waiting for. That feeling that eluded her even during her jump.

A noise of relief and excitement slipped out of her lips as she ran to the kids, scooping them up and kissing the tops of their heads. "I've missed you two so much. Oh, Hugo, how is your arm."

He proudly showed off his cast. "Will you sign it for me, Ms. Mia?"

"Of course, I will. Hadley, how is Belle?"

"She's great. Daddy let her on the counter even though she's not 'posed to go up there."

Mia took a moment to look up at Linc. He was watching her intently, but his face didn't give anything away.

She rose slowly. "Hi," she said softly.

"Hi," he returned.

"Hey, kids, want to come take a closer look at the planes?" Jack asked. "I asked the pilot and he said he would give you a personal tour."

"Can we, Daddy? Can we go?" Hugo was jumping up and down.

Linc smiled. "Yes, but keep those hats on. It's still cold out today."

"Yay!"

As Jack and Emerson took Hadley and Hugo to see the planes, Grace, Xander and Nadine appeared to make themselves scarce. Mia realized they were giving her time with Linc.

"Hi," she said again.

He smiled. Finally. Her heart fluttered at the sight of his lopsided grin.

She couldn't believe he was here. She wasn't sure why he was, to be honest. Part of her wanted to jump into his arms. Hoping more than anything in the world that he would wrap her up and hold her tight.

Yet, there was another part of her, the part that had grown so much in the last couple of months, that knew a simple hug wasn't going to solve anything. While she'd been up in the plane, she'd freaked out. In the end, she conquered a fear and jumped. Now it was time to overcome a completely different fear.

Mia didn't want to fight with Linc. But she knew that they needed to clear the air. Even if she wasn't going to get a hug from him ever again.

"We need to talk," he said. He shifted from one leg to another.

She took a deep breath. "I'll go first. Linc, I'm sorry. I'm so sorry about Hugo's arm and getting the cats," she said, rushing through her words. "I'm sorry I dragged you into my whole list of adventures, which had nothing to do with you or the kids. But I had to do those things. For myself."

Linc stepped forward and put a finger to her lips. "I understand. I really do." He pushed a hair back from her face. "I'm the one who's sorry, Mia. I was horrible to you." He handed her the bouquet of flowers. They were a mixture of pink and white roses. "Hadley picked these. She said you would love pink."

Mia sniffed the bouquet, more so she would have something to do. "They're beautiful."

"They don't make up for the way I was with you last week."

"It's okay, Linc. I get it."

He shook his head. She realized there were dark circles under his eyes. Mia wondered if he'd been suffering from the same sleepless nights as she was.

"No, I was wrong," he continued. "Very wrong. Hugo's accident had nothing to do with you." He shuffled, kicking at the stones in the parking lot. "It was good that I was in Atlantic City."

"Okayyy," she dragged out, not sure where this was headed.

"Mia, you're looking for someone to have adventures with; someone to travel and explore the world with. There's nothing wrong with that. You should get to have all the experiences you feel like you missed out on."

She nodded but didn't say anything.

"I'm searching for someone to have quiet nights tucking the kids in and then binging a Netflix show." He gestured between them. "You and I are in two very different places."

A lump formed in her throat. "Yes, I suppose we are."

She was starting to get it. The flowers and the sign. Linc was breaking things off with her gently. He would have to be kind about it. But he was right. They were in different areas of life. Only...she wasn't sure she was in the phase she wanted to be in.

Because hanging out with Linc and the kids and then indulging in a television binge-fest sounded amazing to her.

She didn't want to lose him. She didn't want to lose Hadley and Hugo either. They obviously weren't her kids, but that didn't mean she couldn't love them as if they were.

Linc's face fell. "Oh, you agree then."

Determined, Mia straightened her shoulders. She wanted this. Linc, children, security. Sure, there would be things she would want to do. Cooking classes were still at the top of the list. But it would be so much better with Linc at her side.

Now she just needed to convince him.

Mia took a deep breath. "What I don't get though, is how I know we're looking for different things, but I still seem to want you so much."

His eyes darkened, and he nodded slowly. "I know how you feel."

"You do?"

It was like a dam broke and Linc's emotions came spilling out. His face fell and his shoulders relaxed. "Yes. Because I want you just as much. Back in high school I thought about you all the time." He offered a half-laugh. "That was nothing compared to now. Ever since you reentered my life, I feel like a different man."

"Really?"

He took the bouquet from her hands and placed it on a nearby table. When he returned to her, he scooped her up in his arms. "Really," he said. "If you need to take time to be independent and adventurous then you do that. I will wait for you. I'll help you, if you want. I'll even let you push me out of my secure routine from time to time."

Her eyes began burning with tears of happiness. He wasn't here to say goodbye. "Oh, Linc."

"I didn't support you last weekend. I made you feel horrible. Shame on me. But going forward, I will be your biggest fan. You have brought so much back to my life. Things I never thought I would feel again. That I was afraid to feel."

He covered her mouth with his and it was the best kiss of her entire life. It felt so natural to kiss him. So right. This was where she belonged.

"I love you, Amelia Dewitt Reynolds. Mia. My Mia."

"I love you, too," she said, finally allowing the tears to come.

He smiled. "I have something for you."

"You do?"

Reaching in his pocket, he handed her a box in the familiar light blue shade of Tiffany's, wrapped with a pristine white bow. She didn't care what was in it. Just seeing that color sent thrills through her.

"Come on, open it," Linc urged.

She undid the bow and removed the lid. Seeing what was inside made her pause. "Um, Linc?" she asked. If she wasn't mistaken, she was looking at the same sterling silver circle necklace that she currently had hanging around her neck. The necklace she'd been given back in high school for her sixteenth birthday.

"Do you like it?" he asked, amusement on his face.

"You know, I do like it." She touched her necklace. "I think you know I like this necklace. Um, however, that doesn't mean I need two of them."

He chuckled. "Look closer."

She did, and at first she saw no difference. It was the same silver chain and circle medallion with a letter inscribed. Then, she realized what she was seeing. Unlike her current necklace with an A for Amelia, Linc had bought her one with an M for Mia.

"Oh, Linc."

"You are my Mia, and I thought you should have the appropriate jewelry to reflect that." He removed the necklace from the box and clasped it around her neck.

She wanted to cry.

"You should keep both of these necklaces. If you want to be Mia one day, great. But maybe you are feeling like Amelia another day. My point is that you shouldn't have to limit yourself." He ducked his head. "I almost made you decide."

"Linc, you didn't."

"What I really want for you is to have the world; anything you want."

"I don't want the world. I want you. And I want the two of us to have experiences together. I want Hadley and Hugo too. I want them to know they are loved and safe."

His eyes glistened. "Seriously?"

"Oh, yes. Me, you, the twins, the kittens."

"A future."

He grabbed her hand. Together, they walked toward the kids and that future.

Epilogue

"It's my wedding day!" Hadley shouted from across the room.

Mia couldn't help but laugh. Neither could her mother, Grace, or Nadine.

"Are you sure it's your wedding day?" Nadine asked. "I thought it was Ms. Mia's day."

Hadley shook her head. "It's my day too."

"That's right," Mia said. "We're all becoming a family today."

"You won't be Ms. Mia anymore. You'll be…Mommy." Hadley covered her mouth and giggled.

Hadley was even more excited than usual. They all were. It had been a year and a half since Linc had reentered her life. Now it was their wedding day.

They were hanging out in the bridal suite at the hotel, sipping champagne—and a Shirley Temple, Hadley's favorite new drink. Nails had been painted, hair had been styled, makeup had been applied. Mia's beautiful ivory dress was hanging on the curtain rod, the summer sun shining on it and making it look even more angelic. Hadley's matching flower girl dress hung next to it.

"Okay, be kind, everyone," Emerson said, emerging from the other room wearing her pink bridesmaid dress.

Mia took in her sister. Her auburn curls were pinned up and her makeup was just enough. She was absolutely glowing.

"You look beautiful," Mia said, crossing to her sister.

"Oh please. I look like a giant beached whale."

"A beached whale wearing the most gorgeous pink dress," Grace added.

"Gee, thanks," Emerson said.

Mia rubbed her hand over Emerson's large belly. "You look pregnant and glorious."

"You mean pregnant and fat?"

Mia laughed. "Em, you're due in a month. Give yourself a break."

"Fine. But at your next wedding, I swear I'm not going to be pregnant again."

"There's not going to be another wedding. Linc is it for me." He was her person, the man she'd been waiting for. Each day proved even more how amazing he was.

"Then I say it's time to get you in that dress," Beatrice said, walking to her daughters and enveloping them both in a hug.

Grace checked her watch delicately. "Oh, yes, we're running slightly behind schedule."

"Thank you for planning this, Gracie. You did an amazing job. I feel like your wedding was just yesterday."

"It was six months ago and I'm still basking in it. Now, stop stalling and get your butt in that dress."

"Yay!" Hadley said. "We get to put our princess dresses on now?"

"You bet, sweetie," Mia said. She was as excited as Hadley to put on her "princess dress."

A half hour later, everyone was in their appropriate dresses, makeup and hair was retouched, and Mia took one last fortifying breath. Then they made their way downstairs. The ceremony would be held at a gazebo in the back of the hotel, which overlooked the Potomac River. They had timed it so they would catch the setting sun. After they said I Do, everyone would move into the stylish ballroom for the reception and dancing.

She and Linc had braved the dance floor again. They revisited the site of Linc's twisted ankle and took classes on both salsa and ballroom dancing. Not only were they ready to let loose at the reception, but they had a special dance prepared for their first turn as husband and wife.

Husband and wife.

Mia felt a thrill at that thought. She couldn't believe how much her life had changed in two short years. She went from a passionless first marriage to a quest to discover herself. In the meantime, she'd found Linc. And now she was becoming his wife and mother to Hadley and Hugo.

"You look absolutely breathtaking, Amelia," her dad said as he met all of the women at the bottom on the stairs.

Grace donned her headset, and lightly prodded Mia's mom, Emerson, Nadine, and Hadley into the foyer that led out to the gardens.

"Thanks, Daddy. I hope you're proud of me."

He kissed her cheek. "I couldn't be prouder. I love you."

"I love you, too," she said, holding back tears.

Nadine took her seat and Beatrice was led to her spot by Jack. Emerson offered one last hug and then made her way down the aisle. Mia couldn't resist peeking out the doors to watch Hadley take her trip. She'd been practicing for a month, and she did an excellent job sprinkling rose petals on her way. When she dropped a particularly large clump, the crowd laughed. At the end of the aisle, Hadley turned around and blew a kiss. This was greeted with a round of applause.

Mia took one more deep breath. She closed her eyes and thought, *I'm getting married!* Then, she had no more time to think because the music started playing.

"That's our cue," her dad said. "Ready?"

"Oh yes."

She took her dad's offered arm and the double doors opened as if on their own. She stepped out into the warm air. The light was beginning to fade, and the sky was streaked with an array of reds, pinks, and oranges. It couldn't be a more perfect summer day.

As she began walking down the aisle, she saw familiar faces. Looking toward the gazebo, her sister had tears in her eyes and Hadley was practically jumping up and down. Hugo stood next to his dad, looking so handsome in his little tux.

Then she saw Linc. Her breath whooshed out of her.

They connected gazes. Linc's eyes were full of tears and Mia knew hers were the same. She couldn't see anything but him. Her handsome groom waiting for her. The walk to the gazebo felt like it took a million years.

Finally, she reached him. Linc and her father shook hands. Then her fingers grasped on to Linc's and squeezed.

"Mia," he whispered. "I've never seen anything more beautiful in my life."

"I love you," she said.

"I love you, too."

Mia looked out at the crowd of smiling faces; all the people she loved. Her parents were beside themselves at becoming grandparents. Her dad had decided to retire in the next year, and her mother was even talking about reducing her hours at Dewitt Bridal.

Grace and Xander had gotten married in the most romantic ceremony in Disney World. Grace truly resembled a princess as she's recited her vows. Her wedding planning business had grown leaps and bounds too. She'd hired on two new people.

She wasn't the only one with a succeeding business. Both Emerson's event planning business and Jack's bar were doing amazing. Emerson had hired a fulltime employee and two-part timers. They were happily nesting, preparing for the baby, and enjoying their dog.

The award they won in Atlantic City was just the beginning for Something True. The website had grown by leaps and bounds. Mia had moved into a marketing and communications position, and they had four new people on staff.

At the end of the day, she had Linc, and the kids. They'd even discussed the idea of having one or two of their own at some point.

She touched a hand lightly to her stomach now. She smiled. "Some point" was now. Only, she hadn't told her groom yet. She thought the wrapped pregnancy test would make for a nice wedding present.

Linc narrowed his eyes. "What's that smile for?"

"You'll find out soon enough."

The minister cleared his throat. "Are you ready to begin?"

Mia had never been more ready for anything in her life.

Her journey had certainly seen its fair share of twists and turns. But ultimately, it led her to exactly where she was supposed to be. Finally, she found her own happy ending with Linc. Her something true.

The End

About the Author

Award-winning romance author Kerri Carpenter writes contemporary romances that are sweet, sexy, and sparkly. When she's not writing, Kerri enjoys reading, cooking, watching movies, taking Zumba classes, rooting for Pittsburgh sports teams, and anything sparkly. Kerri lives in Virginia with her family. For the latest updates on her books or to see pictures of her adorable dog, Harry, visit Kerri at any of the places below:

Website
www.kerricarpenter.com

Facebook
https://www.facebook.com/authorkerri

Instagram
https://www.instagram.com/authorkerri

Twitter
https://twitter.com/authorkerri

If you liked The Daddy Project, make sure you check out books 1 & 2 in the **Something True** series:

The Dating Arrangement
The Wedding Truce

Also by Kerri Carpenter…
Seaside Cove Series
Come What Maybe

Bayside Blog Series
Falling for the Right Brother
Bidding on the Bachelor
Bayside's Most Unexpected Bride

The Wrong Man Series
Kissing Mr. Wrong
Tempting Mr. Wrong

Other Romantic Comedies by Kerri Carpenter
Her Super-Secret Rebound Boyfriend
Flirting with the Competition